Station Nord

GREENLAND SEA

SIORAPALUK

BAFFIN BAY

UPERNAVIK

GREENLAND

ICEL

REY

ILULISSAT

DAVIS STRAIT

ISLAND

NUUK

LABRADOR SEA

Station Nord

GREENLAND SEA

SIORAPALUK

BAFFIN BAY

UPERNAVIK

GREENLAND

IC

ILULISSAT

DAVIS STRAIT

N ISLAND

NUUK

LABRADOR SEA

TRAVELS WITH **GANNON & WYATT**

GREENLAND

PATTI WHEELER & KEITH HEMSTREET

GREENLEAF
BOOK GROUP PRESS

Published by Greenleaf Book Group Press
Austin, Texas
www.gbgpress.com

Distributed by Greenleaf Book Group

For ordering information or special discounts for bulk purchases, please contact Greenleaf Book Group at PO Box 91869, Austin, TX 78709, 512.891.6100.

Design and composition by Greenleaf Book Group
Cover design by Leon Godwin & Greenleaf Book Group
Cover illustration by Leon Godwin
Cover image: Gannon and Wyatt are dressed in synthetically insulated coats with faux-fur trim.

Publisher's Cataloging-In-Publication Data
Wheeler, Patti.
   Travels with Gannon & Wyatt. Greenland / Patti Wheeler & Keith Hemstreet.—First edition.
   pages : illustrations ; cm
   Summary: Upon arriving in Ilulissat, Greenland, Gannon and Wyatt prepare for a dogsled expedition in the Arctic. But before the explorers even crack a whip, they receive a desperate mayday call from an Inuit family that is stranded in the far north. Suddenly, Gannon and Wyatt's expedition to study climate change and Greenlandic culture turns into something far more dangerous—a mission to save lives.
   Interest age level: 007-012.
   Issued also as an ebook.
   1. Twins—Juvenile fiction. 2. Rescues—Greenland—Juvenile fiction. 3. Inuit—Greenland—Juvenile fiction. 4. Climatic changes—Greenland—Juvenile fiction. 5. Adventure and adventurers—Greenland—Juvenile fiction. 6. Greenland—Juvenile fiction. 7. Twins—Fiction. 8. Rescues—Greenland—Fiction. 9. Inuit—Greenland—Fiction. 10. Climatic changes—Greenland—Fiction. 11. Adventure and adventurers—Greenland—Fiction. 12. Greenland—Fiction. 13. Adventure stories. 14. Diary fiction. I. Hemstreet, Keith. II. Title. II. Title: Travels with Gannon and Wyatt. Greenland IV. Title: Greenland

PZ7.W5663 Gre 2014
[Fic]   2014938600

ISBN 13: 978-1-62634-120-3

Part of the Tree Neutral® program, which offsets the number of trees consumed in the production and printing of this book by taking proactive steps, such as planting trees in direct proportion to the number of trees used: www.treeneutral.com.

Printed in the United States of America on acid-free paper

TreeNeutral

14 15 16 17 18 19   10 9 8 7 6 5 4 3 2 1

First Edition

We borrow the earth from our children.
—*Inuit Proverb*

Sometimes a person needs a story more
than food to stay alive.
—Barry Lopez, author of *Arctic Dreams*

ENGLISH/GREENLANDIC:
TRANSLATION OF COMMON PHRASES

Hello—Aluu

How are you?—Qanorippit?

I am well—Ajunngilanga

What is your name?—Qanoq ateqarpit?

Yes, please—Qujan

Thank you—Qujanaq

Greenland—Kalaallit Nunaat

Dog—Qimmeq

It is cold—Issippoq

It is very cold—Issi

CONTENTS

PART I

CAN'T JUDGE A PLACE BY ITS NAME

GANNON

MARCH 30

Greenland? I mean, come on. Has to be one of the most misleading names of any place on the planet.

There's nothing really green about it as far as I can tell. It's an island of rock and snow and ice and not a whole lot else. There aren't any trees, that's for sure. No bushes even. The landscape is gray and white just about everywhere you look. That's not to say that Greenland isn't spectacular. It's much more than that really.

Wyatt and I are settled for the night in a simple hut on the north side of Nuuk, "the world's smallest capital city." Though, I have to say, calling this settlement at the end of the world a "city" is somewhat of a stretch. I mean, this place is so far off the beaten path they don't even have any security at the airport. When I walked off the plane I asked the flight attendant to point me in the direction of customs and immigration. She just laughed. Turns out there is no customs or immigration. No airport police even. Now, I've been to some small and remote places before, but I've never seen that anywhere.

Nuuk does have two stoplights. They're both on the same street and happen to be the only two stoplights in the entire country. So, I guess by Greenlandic standards that qualifies Nuuk as a bustling metropolis. If you add everyone up, about 16,000 people live in the capital, mostly in blocky style apartment buildings and a few picturesque little neighborhoods with colorful homes that gaze out over the icy waters of the Davis Strait.

As I write, the walls of our hut creak and groan under the strain of an angry wind that's coming off the water like a screaming freight train. Cold air sneaks through a crack in the double-paned window next to my desk, numbing my fingers to the bone. An old, rusty radiator clanks and hisses in the corner, struggling to put off enough heat to keep the room comfortable.

Down along the shoreline, chunks of ice have washed up on the rocky beachhead. Out past the ice is deep water, white-capped by the gale. A lone iceberg floats way off in the distance, a glowing white formation that looks like a pair of angel's wings rising out of the dark sea. At the far end of the fjord, towering thousands of feet above the water, is a steep granite mountain face with a jagged, shark-fin point on one end.

It's like I said before, Greenland is more than spectacular!

Wyatt just came back into the hut with his teeth chattering like a jackhammer and said, "It's f-f-f-f-fourteen degrees outside."

Not exactly balmy. And since it's late afternoon already, my guess is that we've reached the high temp for the day. I mean, there's really no way around it, it's just plain cold. And here's the thing: We haven't even crossed the Arctic Circle yet!

Leading up to our trip, my mom suddenly kicked into 'teacher of the year' mode and gave us all these reading and writing assignments to do before we left, which I guess is understandable since we're going to be gone for the better part of two months and all, but I can't say I was super excited about it. Like most kids my age, I can think of a million things I'd rather be doing than schoolwork, but turns out there was some really great reading material on that list. My favorite was the journal of polar explorer, Knud Rasmussen, who crisscrossed the Arctic by dog sled in the early 1900s.

A plaque honoring Knud Rasmussen

Of course, Wyatt and I have a huge amount of respect for the great explorers of the past, explorers who risked life and limb in search of answers to the unknown. Naturally, reading up on Mr. Rasmussen's adventures totally inspired me. I even brought a copy along to keep me company when we're all hunkered down on the ice sheet. Here's a passage he wrote way back in 1917:

```
When I was a child I used to hear an old
Greenlandic woman tell how, far away North,
at the end of the world, there lived a people
who dressed in bearskins and ate raw fish.
Their country was always shut by ice, and
the daylight never reached over the tops of
```

their high fjords. Even before I knew what
traveling meant, I determined that one day I
would go and find these people.

Well, just like Mr. Rasmussen, I want to find these people
of the far North, these descendants of the ancient Eskimos.
I want to learn about their traditions and beliefs and rituals. I want to witness with my own eyes their way of life. I
mean, this is a culture thousands of years old that over the
last century has all but vanished. Basically, by the time we've
covered our last mile by dogsled, it is my goal to have a real
understanding of what it's like to live as the Greenlanders do.

This business of polar exploration has its risks, no question about that. For instance, there's the risk of frostbite, or
worse, freezing to death. We could fall into a crevasse, get
lost in a storm, or go snow blind. We could get sick or swept
away by a roaring glacial river, or the dogs could get hurt,
stranding us on the ice. Heck, we could stumble across a
grumpy old polar bear that doesn't take kindly to us trespass-
ing on his turf.

Okay, I sure hope this isn't some kind of omen, but just
down the hill from our hut is a big cemetery with all these
bright white crosses arranged in perfect rows. There have to
be a few hundred of them, and every single one has a set of
colorful plastic flowers at the base, quivering in the blue-
gray light. Now, I'm trying to keep my thoughts positive
and all, but that's a pretty tall order when you're staring out
the window at a cemetery. To be totally honest, I can't help

wondering how many of the people lying under those little white crosses met their end on an Arctic expedition just like the one we're about to embark on.

All right. Enough of all that. I'm starting to scare myself stupid. Let's just hope we're strong enough to endure whatever the Arctic may throw at us. After all, last thing anyone wants is to end up under one of those little white crosses. But, let's be honest, any time you go on an expedition like this there is a chance that's exactly where you'll end up.

Crosses in the cemetery

WYATT

For as long as I can remember, I have been fascinated by polar exploration. When I was about six or seven, I used to dress up in a fur jacket and run around in the snow with our golden retrievers, pretending to be an explorer on a dangerous Arctic mission. When I got a little older, I started reading the journals of famous polar explorers from the Arctic and Antarctic—Amundsen, Peary, Scott—all incredible tales of bravery and endurance in the most inhospitable environment on earth. These stories really captured my imagination, and so I became determined to one day travel in their footsteps, or to put it more accurately, in their sled tracks. Tomorrow, my brother and I will finally get that chance.

The polar regions of our planet are changing. Temperatures are rising. And in Greenland, temperatures are rising more rapidly than anywhere else. According to the latest scientific data, the average temperature has risen about 2°C (3.6°F) in the Arctic over the last fifty years. That's more than double the global average. It may not seem like much, but the effect is significant. The sea ice in Greenland is disappearing much earlier in the spring than it used to, impacting how the Greenlanders hunt for food. And sea levels are rising, putting coastal areas around the world at risk.

There are many different theories as to what is causing this rapid change in climate. We do know one thing for sure: Our way of life contributes. The pollution we put into the atmosphere speeds up this change.

To aid the Youth Exploration Society in their research on climate change, I will be measuring temperatures on the Greenlandic ice sheet, taking precipitation totals, determining chemical compositions in the air and water, and reporting on the condition of land and sea ice. Basically, I'll be doing all the things Gannon refers to as "excruciatingly boring."

Not for me, though. I love this stuff!

Our parents stayed behind, but they'll be meeting us at the end of the expedition. My dad is finishing up a gallery show of his latest wildlife paintings and my mom is training all the new flight attendants at World Airlines, so she's booked, too. It took some convincing, but given that my brother and I have traveled since we were born, never do anything without expert guides, and have proven time and again that we handle ourselves fairly well in sketchy situations, our parents eventually came around to the idea of us making the journey without them. Besides, they visited Greenland years ago and loved it, so they were really excited about our opportunity to experience the Arctic. I can't say I don't miss them, but it's pretty cool to be on our own for once. No offense mom and dad, but there comes a time when boys must become men. Or, in our case, "young" men.

In December, we began training with mushers at the Toklat Dogsled facility in Snowmass, Colorado, not far from our home. The practice we got controlling sleds over a wide variety of terrain should definitely come in handy when we're on the ice sheet. The entire journey will be just over 800 miles from our starting point east of Ilulissat all the way to Qaanaaq in northern Greenland.

I better wrap up this journal entry. In two hours our flight leaves for Ilulissat, a small town 155 miles (250 kilometers) north of the Arctic Circle. There, we will meet one of our guides, Nuka. A native of Ilulissat, Nuka is seventeen years old and has already participated in several Arctic expeditions. From Ilulissat we'll travel to the ice sheet where we'll meet the sled dogs and Nuka's uncle Unaaq, our lead guide.

How things go once we're on the ice, be it good or bad, this journal will show.

GANNON
APRIL 1

Aerial View of Greenland's Ice Sheet

Well, it's official. I'm talking, officially official. We are in the Arctic! Our feet planted firmly on frozen ground well above the Arctic Circle.

Jeez, I'm so pumped up I don't even know where to begin! Okay, maybe I'll start with the fact that I've never seen so much ice in all my life! I know, a ridiculously obvious statement given that we're in the Arctic and all, but there's really no way to exaggerate just how much ice there is here.

This morning we landed in Ilulissat, a town that's a good deal smaller and a lot more picturesque than Nuuk, with all these homes nestled on a rocky hillside, like little wooden boxes painted in bright blues and yellows and reds and oranges. Snow is piled high on rooftops and even higher along the sides of the roads. The fjord is half frozen over and choked up with massive icebergs jutting every which way. The sun is shining bright and the air is clear and crisp and cold enough to make my lungs shudder when I take a deep breath.

From everywhere in Ilulissat, you can hear sled dogs howling. Seriously, it sounds like some kind of sled dog symphony. I can hear them right now, wailing away like wild wolves. If I were to guess, I'd say there are probably more doghouses in this town than people houses. I'm not kidding, they're all over the place! And all around the doghouses are packs of hearty sled dogs, barking and yipping, steam swirling from their mouths as they snap at the sun.

I have to say, this incredibly unique and beautiful scene has stripped the fear right out of me. I actually feel good. Confident. Like I could accomplish anything. Maybe my brain is frozen or something. I don't know. But whatever it is, I've got this real positive feeling about the journey ahead, which is refreshing, given how I'm usually all hung up on worst-case scenarios, potential disasters, and stuff like that.

Earlier, we met one of our guides, Nuka, at a supply store in the center of town. His family has run the store since before he was born and it carries just about everything you could possibly need, from food to clothing to expedition gear. When we walked through the door, wind sent snow dancing across the floor.

"Gannon and Wyatt!" Nuka shouted with a big smile. "Aluu! Qanorippit?"

Now, I never go anywhere without knowing at least a few basic words and phrases in the native language. Nuka spoke fast, but I was pretty sure he'd said, "Hello, how are you?"

Of course, Wyatt didn't have a clue what he'd said and just stood there like a doofus, so I chimed in.

"Ajunngilanga," I said. "Ajunngilatit?" Translation: I am well. Are you well?

"Aap!" he said with a laugh, which means "yes." "Ajunngilanga," he continued, and then kept right on talking and talking.

"Sorry, Nuka, I lost you after Ajunngilanga. Unfortunately, that's about all the Greenlandic I know."

"That's a lot more than most people know," a boy slightly older than Nuka said as he entered the room. "I'm Erneq. Nuka's older brother."

We all shook hands.

"Welcome to Ilulissat, my friends!" Nuka said.

Nuka and Erneq have dark narrow eyes, thick black hair, and round, happy faces. Both are about my height, probably somewhere close to 5' 8" and look to be about the same weight. To be honest, Nuka and Erneq actually look more like twins than Wyatt and me. Nuka's name means "little brother," which makes sense, well, given that he's a little brother and all.

"You have no idea how great it is to be here!" I said. "I honestly feel like I've landed on the moon or something."

Nuka and Erneq both laughed.

"Our town definitely has a lunar look to it," Erneq said.

"Can you guess the meaning of the word Ilulissat?" Nuka asked.

"I'll go out on a limb and say it has something to do with cold or snow."

"You are on the right track. In Greenlandic, Ilulissat means iceberg. Appropriate name, wouldn't you agree?"

"Without a doubt," Wyatt said.

"I received your messages and understand you have done much training with sled dogs this winter. Do you feel prepared for this journey?"

"As prepared as we'll ever be," Wyatt said.

"Excellent. I am sure we'll all do just fine. Now, let's get you fitted with the proper clothing. This sled trip will be done the traditional way, just as you requested."

Erneq was wearing jeans and a down jacket, but Nuka was dressed in the tradition of his ancestors, with a seal skin coat and these big bushy pants and boots made of polar bear fur.

We walked into the back closet and were fitted with clothes the ancient Greenlanders would have been proud to wear. Everything made from the skins and furs of Arctic animals hunted by Nuka's father and uncle, and hand stitched by his mother.

Traditional Arctic clothing

"My mom would probably burst into tears if she saw all these animal furs," Wyatt said.

"It is a necessary part of life in the Arctic," Nuka said. "For thousands of years our people have worn this clothing.

We have great respect for the animals because we owe our lives to them. Without their skins and furs our ancestors would not have been able to survive in this climate. There is nothing warmer."

Our pants are made from polar bear fur and we each have two coats. The first is made of seal skin. That's the base layer. The second is made of caribou fur and has a warm hood. The mittens are also caribou and look like big bear paws. Our fur boots fit snuggly and are lined with sealskin to keep water out. I'm not going to lie, all of these clothes are about as heavy as a sack of rocks and will definitely take some getting used to, but Nuka swore up and down the extra weight wouldn't be a bother once we encountered the real Arctic cold.

"So, how do I look?" Wyatt asked, as he waddled out of the closet.

"Like Sasquatch on a bad hair day," I said.

"Very funny," Wyatt said.

Wearing all that fur around the shop, I broke into a sweat in about five seconds flat and walked out into the frigid air to cool down. Way out in the bay, I saw a little yellow fishing boat navigating icebergs by way of a thin watery passage. Cars, snowmobiles, and dogsleds moved up and down streets coated in ice. Adults were coming and going from work and kids were just getting out of school and everybody was wrapped snuggly in big, puffy outfits. There was a group of kids sledding down a hill and others playing soccer on the snow, all with big smiles on their faces. A few people waved to me as they passed. One thing's for sure, the cold and ice doesn't slow Greenlanders down a bit.

Nuka and Wyatt walked outside. Again, I noticed the dogs. They were going berserk.

"Nuka, do you ever get used to all this barking?" I asked.

"Ilulissat is home to 4,500 people," Nuka said, smiling. "And over 6,000 sled dogs. We have no choice but to get used to it."

A sled dog in Ilulissat

Nuka pointed out the hospital where he was born, a small red building not a whole lot bigger than the average house, and told us all these amazing stories about growing up in the Arctic. For instance, how kids go outside and play year-round, even when it's well below zero. He also talked about how in the summer, when the sun never sets and no one really sleeps much, kids can be found playing soccer at three in the morning on dirt and gravel fields because there's no grass in Ilulissat. Oh, and here's something he told me that's almost hard to imagine: Each winter the people of Ilulissat spend about a month and a half in complete darkness! Basically, from late-November to mid-January the sun never comes up. After all those long, dark days, when the sun finally peeks its head over the horizon just enough to light the sky for a short time, everyone comes outside to sing and dance in celebration. Now that's a party I'd like to see.

After we talked for a while, Nuka and Erneq's mother and father came racing up on a snowmobile and slid to a stop. They were bundled in furs from head to toe, and soft spoken with cheerful faces and a real mellow way about them. Nuka's mother introduced herself as Kunik and nodded politely to us when we told her our names. Erneq said that Kunik means "kiss." I wondered how in the world she came to have such a name, but wasn't about to ask.

"My name is Makaali," the boys' father said with a strong accent. "It is very nice to meet you. May your journey be a safe one."

Makaali then spoke Greenlandic to his sons, saying all this stuff I couldn't understand.

"Okay, then," Nuka said to us, clapping his fur mittens together. "It's time to go meet my uncle, Unaaq. He just radioed my father and said that the sleds are packed and the dogs are ready to run."

Makaali and Kunik drove us to the airport over icy roads in this giant Arctic-mobile with four big, studded tires on either side. Before they left, they gave us all tight hugs and bid us safe travels. Right now we're enjoying the warmth inside while we wait for someone to gas up the helicopter that will take us to the ice sheet. The pilots are out there checking all the gauges and making sure the propeller is screwed on tight and all that good stuff. Of course, I'm all for them taking their time to make sure this old bird is in good shape, but I'm also really anxious to climb aboard because once that propeller starts spinning and we lift off, well, that's when our journey becomes something more. It becomes an adventure!

WYATT
APRIL 1, 3:17 PM
GREENLAND ICE SHEET, 69° 17' N   49° 52' W
8° FAHRENHEIT, -13° CELSIUS
SKIES CLEAR, LIGHT WIND

The 1950s Russian-made Sikorsky helicopter shook violently as it tilted on its side and moved east over the Ilulissat glacier. I tightened my seat belt as we neared the mouth of the glacier, hoping this vintage flying machine wasn't about to fall to pieces. The ice below us was turquoise blue with deep, jagged cracks caused by the glacier's slow movement towards the open water. Finally, the pilot straightened our path and the helicopter steadied as we moved further inland.

Flying over a massive iceberg

Away from the coast, the cracks disappeared and the ice was solid. The pilots took us lower in a hurry, causing my stomach to jump into my throat. As we descended, I caught sight of the dogs below. They were harnessed to the sleds, jumping around and barking with excitement. The pilots hovered just above the surface, inspecting the landing area to make sure it was free of crevasses. Snow curled up off the ice cap as the helicopter descended. We touched down with a thud and almost immediately the door flew open. Standing before us was Nuka's uncle, Unaaq.

"Make sure to grab all of your gear!" he shouted over the propeller. "Once the helicopter leaves, we are on our own!"

We did as Unaaq said, gathering our backpacks and camera equipment before jumping through the doors onto the ice. As soon as we were safely beyond the reach of the propeller, the helicopter rose off the ice, creating a tornado of snow that swirled around us. I shielded my eyes with my forearm and waved to the pilots. They each gave us a salute, tilted the nose of the helicopter forward, and flew off toward the coast.

Sikorsky helicopter

Unaaq approached and gave us each a strong hug.

"My mushers in training!" he said with a smile. "Are you ready to begin our incredible Arctic expedition?"

"We sure are," Gannon said. "It's going to be epic!"

It should be noted, Unaaq did not become our guide by chance. Before Gannon and I were born, my parents traveled to Greenland and enjoyed a weekend of ice fishing near Ilulissat. Unaaq was their guide. He spoke excellent English and taught my parents how to run a sled. They camped over the ice, catching halibut and red fish that they cooked for dinner. My parents were impressed by his knowledge and enjoyed his company so much they insisted he be our guide.

But reaching people in Greenland isn't always easy. They didn't have his address or email and he wasn't listed in any phone directory (we later learned he doesn't even have a phone), so my parents did the only thing they could think of and sent a letter to his hometown, addressed simply:

```
Unaaq (Sled Guide)
Ilulissat, Greenland
```

Since Ilulissat is a small town, we thought, "What the heck, the postman might just happen to know Unaaq the Sled Guide." Sure enough, the letter found him and, shortly after, he wrote back. Lucky for us, he was interested in our proposed expedition and gave us a date and time to call him at his brother's store. Next thing you know, here we are!

On this expedition we will be using traditional wooden

sleds. There are two smaller sleds for Gannon and me, and a much larger sled that will carry Nuka, Unaaq, and most of our supplies. Gannon and I considered sharing a sled, but since it's not everyday we get to sled across the Arctic, we just couldn't resist the urge to each drive our own. And there are obvious advantages to spreading the weight across more sleds and traveling lighter. Especially when we encounter areas where the ice is broken and hard to navigate.

Harnessed by ropes to each of the smaller sleds are six Greenlandic sled dogs. The larger sled is being pulled by twelve dogs. Greenlandic sled dogs are born to run, have incredible endurance, and can function in temperatures as cold as -70°F. For these reasons, they are the best choice for high Arctic sledding.

We also have a traditional seal skin tent and fur blankets to keep us warm at night. Five days of food provisions were flown in yesterday and loaded onto the sleds by Unaaq. Approximately 225 miles north of here is a polar hut Unaaq stocked with additional food and supplies that we'll pick up when we get there. Then, a little more than halfway through our journey, we'll restock again when we spend a couple nights in an Arctic village near the coast. This strategy was designed to minimize what we have to carry with us during each leg of the journey, so that we are not overloading our sleds and putting unnecessary strain on the dogs.

Before we packed our gear onto the sleds, Unaaq gathered us all together and asked for our attention.

"I have something I must tell you before we begin our journey," he said, his face becoming serious. "In the high Arctic is a village called Siorapaluk. The northern most people in the world live there, the Inughuit. They are the true Polar Eskimos. Few in number, they live much like their ancestors, fishing and hunting caribou. Rarely do they have contact with outsiders."

"Are we going to meet them?" Gannon asked.

"I hope so," Unaaq said. "Just before you arrived I received word that several families of Inughuit are in trouble. They traveled far inland to hunt and their dogs became very ill."

"All of the dogs?" Gannon asked.

"It seems strange, but I was told that every one of their dogs is sick. They cannot pull the sleds any further, so the Inughuit are stranded. The weather up north is not good and it is expected to get worse. No one can reach them. They know how to survive on the ice better than anyone, but their hunt so far has been unsuccessful. If the dogs do not improve enough to bring them back to the Siorapaluk, they will soon run out of food."

"Oh, jeez!" Gannon shouted. "We have to do something! We can't just leave them out there to starve!"

"No, we cannot," Unaaq said. "This is your first sled journey and I do not want to put additional pressure on you, but we must do our best to get to them as quickly as possible. I have worked with dogs my whole life and may be able to help them."

"Well, what are we waiting for?" Gannon shouted as he slung a pack onto his sled and started to tie it down. "Let's get going!"

As we raced to pack up, Nuka explained that his uncle Unaaq is one of the best veterinarians in Greenland. He is also one of the only veterinarians in Greenland, but that doesn't change the fact that he is great at what he does. Throughout the country, he is well respected for his knowledge of sled dogs. Nuka is confident that if we can get to them in time, his uncle will be able to determine the cause of their illness and find a remedy.

Our mission to research climate change and Greenlandic culture during the expedition will remain, but these tasks are no longer priority. What's most important is that we get to the Inughuit people and help them before it is too late.

That's all for now.

The race is on.

Time to mush!

Ready to run!

PART II

A LONG JOURNEY OVER ICE

GANNON

A quick crack of the whip and a call of "huughuaq" and we were off! Ahead of us was a great white kingdom under cloudless, blue skies.

I have to admit, starting out I literally couldn't take my mind off the sick dogs and what might happen to the families if they ran out of food, but the truth is that we're still many days away by sled, and there's really nothing we can do until we get there. In the meantime, Unaaq suggested that we concentrate on running the sleds efficiently and covering as much distance as possible each day.

His advice helped me focus on the task at hand, and soon after we started running the dogs my head cleared and a sense of calm came over me. Watching Unaaq steer his sled across the ice, I felt like I'd been magically transported back in time a hundred years. Seriously, this guy's the real deal—a traditional musher, through and through. He's got all this wispy white hair, sticking straight up from atop his head, like it's never been combed, and a patchy white beard on a plump bronze face. Of course, all of his clothes are of the Eskimo vintage, with a worn out, old caribou parka and these big bushy white pants and boots. Oh, and here's the coolest part, dangling from a leather chain around his neck is an impressive collection of polar bear claws.

"A necklace like that would make an awesome souvenir," I said when we stopped for a break, "but I'm guessing you didn't buy it at a gift shop."

"Oh, no," Unaaq said, laughing. "Some of these claws I just happened across. Others I took after fierce battles."

Excuse me? Did he say he took them *after fierce battles*? With polar bears? Okay, if that's what it takes to bring home a necklace of polar bear claws, I can definitely do without.

Anyhow, it pretty much goes without saying, but Unaaq's dogs ran perfectly. I studied his technique hoping to pick up a few tricks from the master. One thing I learned is how to free the dogs when the lines get twisted up or tangled on their legs. This happens from time to time, even to Unaaq's dogs, but it never slowed him down. He'd just grab the rope and sweep it underneath their legs with a flick of the wrist, almost like a jump rope, and the dogs would be free of the snag.

As my dogs ran, divots of snow popped into the air like exploding kernels of popcorn. Nuka watched us and shouted advice as Unaaq ran their sled. Pretty quickly I felt like I had things under control. My ropes remained tight against the sled, without any real slack building up, which kept the ride nice and smooth. Have to admit, I was really surprised how well it was going for me right out of the gate. I mean, when I was training in Colorado I'd been dumped off my sled so many times I lost count, but so far I'm looking like an old pro out here. Not to give myself credit or anything. It was the dogs, not me. They obviously know how to run well together.

As the dogs picked up speed, the hiss of the sled runners slicing through the snow was like music to my ears and I soon found myself totally relaxed. The warm sun lessened the sting of the cold wind against my face and kept me comfortable as we ran. I have to say, the whole experience was about as close to perfect as you can get. Would have been totally perfect, in fact, if I hadn't suddenly caught whiff of that rancid smell, a smell I know all too well. When it hits your nose there's really no mistaking it—dog farts!

I turned my head away, took a deep breath, and almost laughed out loud when I remembered a joke my dad had told during our training in Colorado, "Unless you're the lead dog, the view really stinks!" Couldn't have said it better myself. For whatever reason, the smell is always the worst at the beginning of the run. I don't think that it goes away, exactly. I mean, these dogs fart like it's their job. I think it's just that you get used to it after a while.

Here are some important commands that I learned from Nuka:

"Harru," for "go right."

"Atsuk," for "go left."

"Huughuaq" means "get going" or "hurry, faster!"

"Kángisârut" means "stop" or "obstacle."

I haven't had a whole lot of time to get to know my dogs yet, but I do know their names. So, let's see, there's Kajoq (brown one), Najaaraq (a brother's little sister, the only female on my team), Anori (meaning wind, for his speed), Turtle (for his slow and steady pace), Olie (meaning just that, Olie), and finally, Kamik (white boots, because he's all black with white fur on his feet). Kamik is the alpha male of the pack. He looks more like a wolf than a dog, with narrow eyes and this brow that's all scowled like he woke up on the wrong side of the sled. And never in my life have I seen a set of choppers like the ones on this guy. No joke, they're like vampire fangs or something. Let's just say, he's the kind of dog I wouldn't want to get into a scrap with. Might come away missing a hand.

With the exception of Kamik, who is mostly black, all my dogs are white, some with dark streaks on their backs and tails. All of them are built with great, broad chests and strong shoulders. Bottom line, each one is a good, capable snow dog and I'm privileged to have them on my team.

Dog flatulence aside, I now know what Mr. Rasmussen meant when he wrote, "Give me snow, give me dogs; you can keep the rest." Out here, that's exactly how I feel.

The alpha male, Kamik

WYATT

APRIL 1, 9:48 PM
GREENLAND ICE SHEET, 69° 22' N 49° 49' W
16° FAHRENHEIT, -9° CELSIUS
SKIES CLEAR, LIGHT WIND

Chaotic is how I'd describe my sledding today. Inefficient, embarrassing, amateur, pathetic even. Yeah, those words describe it pretty accurately, too.

I'm extremely disappointed in myself. All that time training in Colorado and today I looked like I had never run a sled in my life. For some reason, my dogs refused to run together in any sort of uniform fashion. It was like each dog had its own destination in mind. They continued to leap over one another, tangling themselves in a mess of ropes that looked like, as Gannon put it, "the web of a blind spider." When the ropes got too twisted up to continue, I would have to stop and try to sort them out while they snarled and snapped at me.

Making matters worse, Gannon ran his sled about as well as a native Greenlander. Nuka and Unaaq even complimented how good he was at controlling his dogs. "He's a natural," they said. We're only one day into the journey and Gannon's dogs already seem to love him. It's like he's been their master since they were pups. My dogs on the other hand, they'd just as soon leave me behind.

I can tell that my lead dog, Tooguyuk, isn't very happy about me being in charge. Maybe it's that he's used to Unaaq and Nuka giving orders. Whatever it is, he's giving me some serious attitude. The alpha dog sets the tone, so the rest of the dogs are just as agitated with me as he is. Before we started running the sleds, Unaaq made sure we knew the names of each dog by memory. The rest of my team is made up of Suluk, Jake, Qanic, Ralphy, and Big Foot. They are all males, and I still get some of them mixed up, which could be part of the problem. No one appreciates being called the wrong name, not even sled dogs.

Hopefully, I'll do better tomorrow. If I can't gain control of my dogs, we'll never make it to the Inughuit people in time. Even though I'm slowing us all down, Unaaq and Nuka have been very patient with me, and I am determined to get it right. I have to get it right. There is no other option. Many lives depend on it.

Nuka shows us how to run a sled

GANNON

END OF DAY #1 ON THE ICE

Okay, we just finished setting up our accommodations for the night and I have to say, they're totally awesome! Basically, we've built a replica of an ancient Arctic tent camp. Surprisingly, it wasn't all that hard to do.

What we did first was dig out a square in the snow a couple feet deep and probably ten feet long on each side to give us some protection from the wind. Then we packed the snow hard, set up a tent frame carved out of whalebones, and draped a few sealskins over the top. Nuka's mom stitched the skins to fit the frame perfectly. Last thing we did was throw down a few musk ox furs as flooring and open a narrow shaft in the top so that some fresh air can flow through. The ventilation allows us to burn these small dishes Unaaq packed with seal blubber, which basically burns just like a candle and provides good light. To keep us warm while we sleep, we each have our own thick fur blanket.

Traditional Greenlandic tent

"In the winter, igloos or ice caves are used to protect against the Arctic cold," Unaaq explained. "The snow and ice provides better insulation. Because it is spring and the temperatures are warmer this tent should be all we need."

"What if the weather changes and the temperature drops?" Wyatt asked.

"The tent and furs will protect us in temperatures as cold as minus 20°F. If we encounter lower temperatures, we will build an igloo or ice cave."

Definitely pumped about staying in an igloo at some point, but jeez, I sure hope it doesn't get any colder than 20 below. Today was pretty warm. Almost uncomfortably so. Late-afternoon, I actually broke a sweat, but I'll take a little perspiration over 20 below any old day of the week!

As for the dogs, once we settled on a location for our campsite, we drove metal stakes into the ice and chained each dog up separately. Unaaq explained that it's important to put some distance between each dog. Otherwise, they get on each other's nerves and that leads to all kinds of rough-housing and sled dog roughhousing is pretty serious business. Now, I'm a total animal person, love them to death, especially dogs, so it's hard for me to keep from plopping down in the snow and playing with them like I would a pet, but Nuka told me that I need to gain their trust before I do any of that. Otherwise, I'm asking for trouble.

According to the detail nerd, aka Wyatt, we ran the sleds for five hours today and covered about 19 miles. Not exactly what I'd call *epic*. I know Unaaq said not to think ahead and take our expedition one day at a time and all that, but after only sledding 19 miles today I can't help but worry that we may never get to the Inughuit. I mean, come on! 19 miles? I could've walked farther in snowshoes.

Then again, it is only day one, and technically it wasn't even a half-day, and there were definitely some hiccups along the way (mostly Wyatt's), so maybe 19 miles isn't all that terrible. Anyway, tomorrow is going to be much more challenging, without a doubt. Unaaq said we should have mostly flat ice for a good clip, so our goal is to cover a total of 75 miles. Now, that'll be *epic*!

It helps that we won't have to hunt for food along the way. But in keeping with the Greenlandic tradition, we will get a chance to fish when we visit the Arctic village. Mostly, though, we'll eat the food that was pre-packed, which leads me to tonight's menu. So, for starters we've got some tasty looking caribou jerky, and for the main course some not-so-tasty looking dehydrated salmon with a side of rock hard biscuits. As for beverages, we have a choice—a warm cup of tea or melted snow, straight up.

Mmm, yummy!

WYATT

APRIL 2, 10:17 AM
70° 09' N   49° 05' W
34° FAHRENHEIT, 2° CELSIUS
CLEAR SKIES, NO WIND

In early April at this latitude, sunlight lasts about 15 hours per day. Not much different than what we're used to back home. However, that's about to change dramatically. By the time we reach northern Greenland, around 78°N latitude, we will have close to 24 hours of daylight.

This morning the sun is intense. Its reflection on the ice cap is almost blinding, even through my tinted goggles. The sun and lack of wind make it feel much warmer than the air temperature indicates. I was sweating while I harnessed the dogs and have been running the sled without my fur coat all morning. I'm curious to see just how warm it gets out here today.

For this expedition, I brought along a great new gadget; a barometer, which will help us predict the weather by monitoring the rise and fall of barometric pressure in the atmosphere. To give an example, the pressure right now is at 30.20 millibars and falling rapidly. That means the air temperature should get warmer and the skies cloudier.

Unaaq explained to us that in the spring and summer it can actually be warmer on the ice than it is on the coast. The sun reflects off the ice and warms the air, while the coastal areas are cooled by wind currents that blow off the ocean.

It is still early spring, but we have already come across large pools of ice melt.

Puddles on the ice sheet

"It's unusual to have this much standing water so early in the spring," Unaaq said, as we navigated what seemed like hundreds of puddles. "Warm weather seems to come a little earlier every year. Last summer more Arctic sea ice melted than ever before. This year it looks like the warming cycle will continue."

The warmth just increases the urgency to get north as quickly as possible. It should be colder, the ice more solid. Running the sleds through slush is hard work. The good news is that I have the commands down pretty well now and

I've finally gained some control of the dogs. I'm using a more authoritative voice and have learned to crack the whip with a loud snap, which also helps keep them in line. All in all, I'm more confident that we'll actually make it to northern Greenland and the Inughuit. I just hope we make it there in time to help.

GANNON
DAY #3 ON THE ICE CAP

Warning: Crevasse!

When I looked into the crevasse, I got so dizzy my legs almost gave out. For real, I felt like I was about to fall over and go tumbling into the crack. And this thing was deep. Like, disappear-into-the-center-of-the-earth deep. There was all this snowmelt flowing through the upper section of the crevasse and cascading over the edge into an abyss. I stepped back behind Unaaq and knelt down.

Luckily, the dogs slowed down ahead of the crevasse without me even giving a command. I just figured they were getting tired and needed some rest since we'd been running them hard for hours through wet snow. But they definitely knew something wasn't right. Eventually, they came to a complete stop and got all tangled up in the ropes. I cracked the whip a few times and told them to stop loafing, but they weren't having any of it. They just stared at me with these scowls on their faces, almost like they were trying to say, "Trust us, buddy. You don't want to go any farther!"

On the ice cap, the entire surface is white and mostly flat and that makes it hard to spot crevasses until you're literally right on top of them. Unaaq shouted for all of us to stay put, as he and Nuka hopped off their sleds and went to check things out. About thirty or so feet ahead, they both stopped and knelt down. Walking up behind them, I could hear the rush of the water, and next thing I know there's this massive crack right in front of me, probably ten feet across, if not wider.

"This is a moulin," Unaaq said, pointing to the blue hole that sank deep into the ice. "A moulin is a tunnel that goes all the way to the bottom of the ice cap."

"And how far would that be?" I asked.

"The ice here is two miles thick," Unaaq said.

"Two miles thick?" Wyatt asked. "As in 10,560 feet?"

I rolled my eyes. Drives me nuts when my brother tries to act all smart.

"That's right," Nuka said.

"And this is why I only travel by dogsled," Unaaq said. "If we had been on snowmobiles, we might not have seen the crevasse until it was too late. Sled dogs are brave, strong, and most importantly, they sense things we do not."

"I was about to scold them for getting all tangled up in the ropes," I said. "But I should be praising them. They just saved our lives!"

"They sure did. They are good dogs, aren't they?"

"Good dogs? Sorry, but that's a major understatement. Dogs that save my life aren't just good dogs, they're the most awesome dogs ever!"

WYATT

APRIL 3, 6:42 PM
40° FAHRENHEIT, 4° CELSIUS
ELEVATION: 10,560 FEET (2 MILES HIGH)
DISTANCE COVERED TO DATE: 137 MILES

Never could I have imagined a glacial lake as big as the one we saw today. It looked like a glowing blue gem sitting atop the ice sheet, so vast it could have easily been mistaken for a sea. The water was crystal clear and we could see the bottom.

Along it were black marks where something called 'cryoco-nite' had settled.

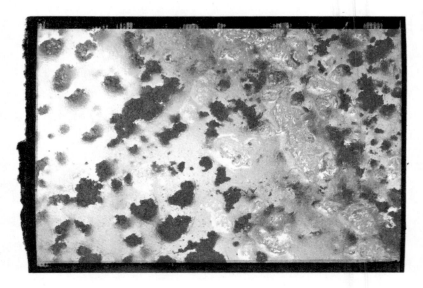

Cryoconite on the ice

"Cryoconite is pollution carried to the Arctic by the wind," Unaaq explained. "It is made up of volcanic soot, fires, coal burning fuel, and other pollutants that come from as far away as Europe, North America, and Asia."

Looking around, I noticed for the first time the black marks that were staining the white landscape. It is amazing to see the impact of air pollution in a place where there are no factories, no cars, no real way of creating any kind of air pollution at all. It seems the Arctic is an innocent victim of the pollution we create in other parts of the world.

"You know," Gannon said, "I've been sweating so much today I'm honestly thinking about taking a dip. You have to admit, the water looks really refreshing."

Unaaq and Nuka laughed.

"It does, but I wouldn't recommend it," Unaaq said.

"Why not?"

"Well, it is melted ice, for one. So it is extremely cold. More importantly, a split could open in the ice and drain this lake very quickly. And, trust me, you do not want to be anywhere near the lake when it goes. Especially not swimming in it."

"You'd be like a small toy getting sucked down the drain of a bathtub," I said.

"It would definitely be an exciting ride," Nuka said, with a chuckle, "but it would be your last."

"Okay, I get the point," Gannon said. "No swimming."

We stood quietly for few minutes, just staring out over the glacial lake while the harsh Arctic sun beat down on us from above.

"Kiappoq," Unaaq said, fanning his coat as he eyeballed a path around the lake.

"Kiappoq means it's warm," Gannon said to me.

"I think I could have figured that out," I shot back.

"Could you have?" he asked, raising his eyebrows.

"Yes, I could have."

"Mmm, I'm not so sure about that."

Amazing. Even in the middle of nowhere Gannon finds a way to get on my nerves.

After dinner, clouds came and there was a brief period of misty rain. I did not expect rain this high in the Arctic. Not in early April. This time of year, it should still be cold enough that all precipitation falls as snow. Again, I'm surprised by the warmth this far north. Nuka and Unaaq seem just as surprised. They are actually worried that we might get stuck out here, surrounded on all sides by a massive sea of ice melt! And if they are worried, I'm worried.

Witnessing these massive pools makes me wonder: What if the Arctic ice were to melt? I'm talking all of it. What would that do to sea levels around the world? Would coastal cities be completely flooded? Would it be just like one of those Hollywood doomsday films where the skyscrapers in New York City get half submerged by a tidal surge? It seems unlikely, but given all the melt we've seen I can't help but wonder if something like that could actually happen one day.

The Greenlandic ice sheet alone is more than 1.7 million square kilometers (656,000 miles), which is almost 2½ times the size of Texas. It covers over 80 percent of the country and is two miles thick in some places. Scientists note that the Greenland ice sheet has shrunk at an alarming rate over the past few decades. The polar ice cap, which covers much of the Arctic Ocean, is melting, too. Most climatologists say that it is only a matter of time before there isn't any sea ice at the North Pole during the summer months. These are major changes that we can't ignore. I really don't know what can be done, but it will be the responsibility of our generation to figure out a solution and prepare for what might lie ahead, just in case nature gives us no other option but to conform.

Inland ice moving out to sea

GANNON
EVENING

Today we got to our supply depot and thank goodness for that because the meat we had for the dogs was almost gone (thanks to the extra helpings I've been giving them), and our rations were running low, too. No joke, I felt like I was about to pass out from hunger, so it sure was a sight for sore eyes to step into that bear-proof hut and see that huge stockpile of food. There was salami and jerky and nuts and noodles and canned vegetables and fruits and some curry powder to give an extra boost of flavor to whatever we cook. It was like a little Arctic mini-mart in there!

"How the heck did you get all this stuff out here, Unaaq?" I asked.

"A very big sled and a lot of dogs," he said.

"Well, I don't mean to be impatient, but I'm drooling at the sight of all this food. So, what do you say we get the dogs fed ASAP and get on with stuffing ourselves silly?"

"Good plan," Wyatt said.

So that's what we did, quickly feeding the dogs a hearty meal and gathering around a little table inside the hut to enjoy a feast of feasts. Unaaq brought us a healthy sampling of foods from the shelf, while Nuka, Wyatt, and I snatched it all up before he even had a chance to put it on the table.

"Mmm, that looks good," I said, grabbing an unlabeled aluminum can from his hands.

"What is it?" Wyatt asked, his cheeks swollen with food like a chipmunk.

"Doesn't matter," I said, peeling back the lid to find a can packed with diced carrots, green beans and corn, all bright and colorful and delicious looking.

"Anyone mind if I polish off this entire can?" I asked.

"Help yourself," Unaaq said. "There is plenty more for all of us."

I turned the can up, pretty much inhaling the veggies as they spilled into my mouth. After that, I tore into a strip of beef jerky, then some kind of dehydrated fruits, then this chewy thing that stuck to my teeth and tasted real smoky. Half the time, I wasn't even sure what I was eating. Didn't matter. It all tasted delicious.

By the time the feast was over we could hardly move we were so full and ended up lying around in the sun for a good fifteen minutes or so before we packed up the rest of the food and continued on. What's crazy is that I'm already hungry again, and it's only been a few hours! My brother the brainiac says we're burning something like 6,000 calories a day out here, so I guess we're almost always going to be hungry, no matter how much we eat.

Speaking of Wyatt, man did he pull a boneheaded move this afternoon. A couple miles past the hut nature called, so Wyatt stopped his sled to relieve himself. What he didn't realize was that one of the sled ropes had somehow gotten twisted around the belt on his polar bear pants. Well, just as he finished turning the snow yellow a couple of his dogs got in a bit of a tussle. So, what does Wyatt do? He accidentally yells "huughuaq" (go) instead of "kángisârut" (stop) and the dogs take off like a shot, dragging my poor brother alongside the sled.

He went zipping by on his back like a horse jockey being dragged down the final straight away at the Kentucky Derby. Think he might have been yelling, "Help!" but I was laughing so hard I couldn't really tell for sure. Nuka caught up with him and brought the dogs to a stop, but not before Wyatt's ego had been banged up pretty good. No denying it, the kid's done some lame-brained things in his day, but that ranks up there in the top five. Maybe top three. Lucky for him I didn't have my video camera handy. When I think about it, it's tragic, really. It would have been the most hilarious video footage ever!

WYATT

APRIL 4, 7:41 PM
72° 57' N   51° 05' W
35° FAHRENHEIT, 3° CELSIUS
SKIES CLEAR

I was in a pretty foul mood and ticked off at Gannon for reasons I won't mention and thinking of how I could get him back when suddenly, a fight broke out between Too-guyuk and Big Foot. These two have gotten in minor scraps before, but this was different. This was a fight to the death!

Big Foot is the second largest dog on my team, a young and strong male, and he was challenging Tooguyuk. Survival instincts passed down for thousands of years took control and they attacked one another with jaws wide and snapping. Unaaq and Nuka ran over to break it up, but the dogs were insane with rage and oblivious to the whips cracking atop their backs. They were up on their hind legs, lunging forward with their front paws, their jaws striking out at one another's jugulars. Fighting his way in between them, Unaaq shouted and tried to break them apart. He took the handle of his whip and brought it down repeatedly atop the dogs. Finally, the dogs acknowledged Unaaq's presence. He was the true alpha male. The master. And the dogs had been trained well enough to know that you never challenge the master.

Big Foot had a deep gash over his nose and bright red blood was smeared across his face, making it clear who had won the fight. Bowing in defeat, Big Foot took a position away from the rest of the pack. Unaaq tended to him, cleaning and bandaging the wound. I helped Nuka inspect Tooguyuk for injuries, but we found none.

All things considered, it could have been worse. Much worse. At least my dog team is still intact. Maintaining the health of the team is critical given the great distance we are attempting to cover on our expedition.

In four and a half days we have traveled a total of 248 miles. That's an average of 55 miles per day. Taking into account that we ran dogs for approximately 12 hours each full day, and 5 hours on the half-day, we're averaging a speed of 4.7 miles per hour. That's not bad. It's not great either, but overall I'm happy with our pace.

Earlier, we radioed the village of Siorapaluk to report our

coordinates and check on the weather. Our contact there is a woman named Suunia.

"How are the skies looking north of us?" Unaaq asked her.

"The weather looks good for you," Suunia said. "It should be clear sledding for a good stretch. Temperatures will become colder over the next few days, but you shouldn't run into any storms until you are much further north."

Just the kind of weather report I was hoping to hear. The possibility of becoming surrounded on all sides by ice melt is now much less of a concern.

"We're going to stay in a village about one hundred miles north of Upernavik," Unaaq told Suunia. "There we will resupply so we can bring plenty of food to the Inughuit and their dogs. How are they holding out?"

"A small rescue team from Qaanaaq braved the storm and was able to reach them," Suunia said. "They could not figure out what has made the dogs so ill, but the team was able to bring a few of the youngest children back to the village safely."

"That's wonderful to hear!" Nuka said.

"The weather is getting worse and the rescue team will not be able to return for the others until it clears. It would take several helicopters to bring everyone back and all flights are grounded. We are very worried. Some of the elders are not doing so well and I don't think the dogs will last much longer without a remedy for their illness."

"You said the dogs have not eaten anything unusual or come in contact with other animals?" Unaaq asked. "No scuffles with Arctic foxes or wolves?"

"As far as I know, they have kept a normal diet and stayed out of trouble."

"Okay. We are on our way and will do our best to help when we arrive."

"We cannot thank you enough, Unaaq. May your travels be safe."

GANNON
APRIL 8

Way down the hill at the end of a fjord, I spotted all these little white domes that looked like bubbles pushing up through the surface of the snow. There were also several miniature homes sitting on the ice, painted red and perfectly square with triangular roofs.

"The Arctic village!" I yelled. "Atsuk! Atsuk!" and cracked the whip hard against the cold, brisk air.

The dogs obeyed my command and turned left down the slope, running towards the village with a renewed energy. I'm pretty sure they were as excited to get there as I was.

"The people in this village have built some modern homes," Nuka had told us before we arrived, "but mostly they continue to live the traditional lifestyle. They want to pass the ancient knowledge on to the younger generation. Most Greenlanders today grow up without that knowledge."

When we arrived we were greeted with curiosity and smiles, and even though Wyatt and I are total strangers, they were quick to smack us on the back affectionately and wrap us up in bear hugs like we'd been friends forever. I liked them right away.

Some of the men here are wearing ski jackets and waterproof pants with polarized sunglasses and beanie caps, just like we wear at home. Others are dressed in the traditional style, wearing seal skins and furs.

The simplicity of their lifestyle is really inspiring, and my first impression is that they are some of the happiest people I have ever met. Seriously, I've never seen so many smiles or heard so much laughter, and to be totally honest, I don't even have a clue what they're smiling and laughing about. Wyatt's funny looks would be my first guess. Who knows? Whatever it is, it's plain to see that they really enjoy life.

Being here makes me wonder about all the things we have today—all the products and gadgets and gizmos and whatnot. I mean, do we really need all that stuff? Out on the ice cap, the answer becomes pretty clear. Absolutely, undeniably, and without question, no. When I think about it, food, clothing, and shelter (and for me, maybe a journal), that's all I really need. Pretty much everything else is a "want" not a "need," and there's a big difference between the two.

Okay, have to run. I've been given the thumbs up to take some video around the village and need to get some footage while I have the chance.

Signing off until later . . .

WYATT

The total population of this small encampment is 126 people, ranging in age from 3 months to almost 100 years old. The woman who is nearly 100 just happens to be the great-great-grandmother of the 3-month-old baby. She is hunched slightly, and her face holds a thousand wrinkles that all turn upward when she smiles. This is the first great-great-grandmother I have ever met. Gannon calls her "Triple G."

Right now a bunch of children are being taught to hunt with bows and arrows. This is an important skill that they are encouraged to develop from an early age. And I'm talking a real early age. The oldest kid in the group couldn't be more than 10 and the youngest is probably 4 or 5, tops. One of the fathers built a rabbit and a fox out of snow, and the kids are taking turns shooting arrows at the targets while he coaches them on technique. Arrows are flying every which way, and the kids are all giggling and teasing one another. They may not show much promise yet, but by the time they're old enough to hunt they'll be experts.

We tied up the dogs and set up our tent about 25 meters from the nearest house, but we were encouraged to tour the village and even visit people in their homes. Of course,

Gannon's already making his rounds. I just saw him walk into one of the igloos with his video camera and journal. Boy, do I feel sorry for the poor people inside. They have no idea what they're in for.

GANNON

LATE NIGHT

Okay, Greenlanders might just be the greatest storytellers on the planet. They're definitely some of the most imaginative, that's for sure. What's amazing is that all of their stories have been passed down in the oral tradition from one generation to the next, which basically means the stories are spoken instead of written. How they have all these long, wild stories committed to memory is totally beyond me. I can hardly remember a joke if I don't write it down.

The stories that Unaaq translated from Papik. . . I mean, whoa. They totally blew my mind! Now, Papik is an "Angdkut," which basically means he's a magician or shaman. There really aren't many shaman left in Greenland today. It's a part of the Inuit culture that's all but disappeared. In fact, Unaaq thinks that Papik might be the last of his kind.

Without a doubt, Papik has to be one of the most interesting guys I've ever met. He's got this crazy energy and dances around the village wearing this oversized polar bear fur and barking and growling and swinging seal skin straps around like helicopter propellers. I just about fell over when

Papik told us that he has the power to crawl out of his skin and then back into it.

"Whoa, I'd like to see that," I said.

"I don't think you would," Unaaq said. "It is believed that anyone who sees him do it will die on the spot."

"Oh, jeez. Really?"

"So they say."

"All righty, then. Forget I ever mentioned it."

One of the stories Papik told had us totally cracking up. It's the story of an Arctic giant who was so big that he called the polar bear a fox. One day he saw five men kayaking in the ocean and thought they would make for nice ornaments so he scooped them up. When he returned home, he put the men on his shelf and sat down to admire his new ornaments. Later that night after a feast of polar bear meat the giant fell into a deep sleep. Well, knowing this might be their only chance to get away, the frightened men climbed down from the shelf and escaped. When the giant woke and saw that the men were gone he said, "Oh, dear. This is all my fault. If I had just remembered to pull their eyes out of their heads they would not have been able to escape."

Okay, sure, it's a little creepier than most of the fairy tales I was told growing up, but every bit as entertaining.

As the shaman of the village, the people believe whatever Papik says. Ancient wisdom tells them that if they don't believe in the magicians the animals they hunt will become invisible and they will have no food and will eventually starve. So, yeah, it seems pretty important to believe Papik.

Okay, time for some shut-eye. Just hope an Arctic giant doesn't pluck me from my tent while I sleep.

WYATT
APRIL 9, 10:31 AM
74° 17′ N   56° 06′ W
15° FAHRENHEIT, -9° CELSIUS
SKIES CLEAR, LIGHT WIND

This morning we took the sleds over the tongue of a glacier into the bay. A glacier "tongue" is a long sheet of ice that extends from the coast into the sea. We were led by a man that calls himself Alluaq, which literally means "hole in the ice for fishing."

Right now we are settled atop the sea ice in the middle of a bay surrounded on three sides by barren mountains. When we arrived, Alluaq cleared away a circle of snow. We were all given metal poles with sharp tips, like spears, and began chipping away at the ice. Alluaq said this time of year the ice here is normally two or three feet thick. Today, it's just under one foot thick, which makes me a little nervous to be out so far over the water, but Alluaq's been doing this his entire life, so I've put my faith in him.

Greenland's spectacular scenery

Within the hour, we had a hole carved in the ice about six or seven feet around. Once the hole was cut, Alluaq and Unaaq baited large hooks with meat and lowered it on thick ropes to a depth of 750 meters.

"There are big fish in these waters," Alluaq said. "But they are usually very deep."

Now that the line is baited, we just sit around and wait. And the waiting part is tough given that the clock is ticking for the Inughuit families who need our help. With each passing day, their situation becomes more desperate. We decided that if we don't catch anything today we're going to continue north tomorrow with as much seal and whale meat as the villagers can spare. But they can't spare much. Food is pretty scarce for everyone right now.

Ice Fishing

GANNON

FISH CAMP

"We've got something!" Nuka yelled, waking me from a deep sleep.

I threw off my blanket, jumped to my feet, and got this massive head rush that almost tripped me up as I made my way to the fishing hole. When my head cleared I saw Alluaq with the fishing rope in his hands. He was tugging as hard as he could to pull whatever we'd caught up to the surface. Veins were bulging from his neck and forehead and his face was turning purple. Despite all that effort he wasn't having much luck. Actually, the line was being pulled deeper. For a second, I thought Alluaq was about to get pulled down through the hole into the ocean.

"Wow, this is a big fish," Nuka said. "Let's help Alluaq."

We all grabbed hold of the rope and tugged like crazy, but whatever was on the hook was a lot stronger than all of us combined. No joke, it felt like we were trying to pull a semi-truck from the bottom of the ocean.

Since we couldn't gain an inch, we harnessed all of the dogs to the rope and cracked the whip and got them all digging their paws deep into the snow and pulling like mad. Well, slowly the dogs made progress, but the rope was so long that the dogs just kept going and going. I'm serious, it looked like they would reach the village before the length of rope ran out.

When that beastly looking sea creature finally stuck its head through the hole I almost jumped right out of my boots!

"You've got to be kidding me!" I shouted, still back peddling.

It looked almost like a super-sized catfish, all gray and slimy with a long head and wide mouth.

"What in the world is that thing?" I asked.

"Eqalussuaq," Nuka said.

"Come again?"

"Greenlandic shark. The largest of the Arctic fish. And this is a big one!"

Alluaq yelled something to us in Greenlandic.

"Watch out for its teeth!" Unaaq repeated in English. "They are small, but sharp as razors!"

The dogs looked like they were a mile away and still running to help pull this giant onto the ice.

"Greenlandic sharks will eat just about anything," Unaaq said. "Scientists have found caribou in their bellies. Even polar bears."

"No way," I said.

"Yes way," said Unaaq with a chuckle. "That's why we warn people never to stand too close to a hole in the ice. The Greenlandic shark might be waiting to jump up and snatch you."

"I can see how a warning like that would be effective," I said.

The shark flesh is actually toxic to humans unless it is fermented over a long period of time, but that's just fine by me because I can't say I was all that excited about sampling shark anyhow. Apparently it's a safe and tasty meal for the dogs though, and that's why it's a valuable catch.

When the dogs returned to the fishing hole they could hardly contain themselves, yipping and salivating and tugging at their leashes, just dying to sink their teeth into some shark meat. As Alluaq carved up chunks of meat one of the dogs lunged forward and snatched some right out of his hand. Well, Alluaq wasn't too happy about that and gave the dog a good reprimanding. Dogs are not allowed to eat until their master says so.

This one shark will feed all of their dogs for at least a month, so it frees up some of the fish, seal and whale meat they had stock piled for the dogs, which we will now take to the Inughuit.

That they would go through all this work to keep the dogs fed and healthy just goes to show how important they are to the Greenlanders' way of life. I have to think that if we all had to catch sharks and whales and seals to feed our dogs at home, instead of just scooping them a bowl of dog food, well, dogs probably wouldn't be such popular pets.

We all stood around and watched Unaaq and Alluaq carve up the shark meat, while Unaaq talked a little bit about their strong connection with nature.

"Here in the Arctic, we are one with nature," he said. "If we are in tune with the spirits of nature an animal will willingly give its life for us. It will die so that we can live. That is the animal's purpose and it understands this when we come for it. Without the animals, we all die. That is why we give thanks to the animal before eating its meat and organs. We give thanks for its skin and fur, which we use for clothing and shelter. We even use its bones to make things such as tools, weapons, and frames for housing. Nothing ever goes to waste."

Unaaq made his point crystal clear, using his knife to fish around in a steaming pile of shark innards. In all that mess of intestines, he happened upon a shrimp the shark had swallowed whole. When he stuck it on his knife and extended it to me, I thought he was joking.

"Shrimp cocktail?" he asked, with a huge smile.

"Thank you, but I'll pass," I said.

"Suit yourself," he said and popped the shrimp into his mouth.

I'll be honest, I just about threw up at the sight. But hey, like he said, nothing here goes to waste. Not even the undigested food inside the animal's stomach.

Mmm, yummy!

WYATT
APRIL 9, 8:05 PM

At first, I thought what I heard was a clap of thunder. But when I looked up to the sky there wasn't a cloud to be seen. Immediately following the explosive crack, I heard a low rumble and felt the ice tremble under my feet. The typically slow-moving and calm Alluaq was running, quickly gathering his fishing equipment and throwing it onto his sled. I knew something was terribly wrong.

"The ice is splitting!" Nuka shouted. "We have to move fast!"

Alluaq and Unaaq had just finished packing up the shark meat and were frantically gathering all of their gear. I raced to make sure I had all of my belongings securely tied to my sled and then went for my dogs, harnessing them as fast as I could. They had been in a near frenzy over the smell of shark meat, but had settled and allowed me to rope them to the sled without any hassle. I think they could sense that we were in danger. Once they were tied up, they took off so fast I was barely able to hold on.

The dogs knew exactly where to go. The mainland. If we could just get to land we would be safe. If we didn't get there quickly enough, the ice could break away and set us adrift on the open sea.

To the south, on the horizon, I could see a split forming. It looked like a dark line in the ice and it was getting bigger! Unaaq and Alluaq had jumped on the same sled and were leading us toward a distant mountain, away from the crack. Gannon was right behind them. Nuka, brought up the rear just in case any of us ran into trouble.

From the southern split, I looked east and I noticed another split forming in the sea ice. There were now two fractures moving toward each other. If they were to meet, we would be cut off from the mainland. Stranded on an island of floating ice.

Alluaq and Unaaq steered the dogs back toward the center, running hard for solid ground. It felt like my dogs couldn't run fast enough. I was falling behind. Realizing this, my blood ran cold.

Nuka moved his sled along the side of mine and began shouting at my dogs in Greenlandic. He then pulled ahead, trying to get my team to run faster.

"Go, Tooguyuk!" he shouted. "Faster, faster! Follow me!"

The ice was now almost fully detached from the mainland. There was only a narrow strip that we could sled across and it was getting narrower by the second. I shouted at the dogs.

"Huughuaq! Huughuaq!"

They bore down and ran as hard as they could, sprinting for that bridge of ice. Alluaq and Unaaq took their sleds right over it without any problems. Gannon was next and made it with just a few feet to spare on either side, but the fracture was opening up fast, creating a channel of water as it moved. Nuka looked back at me and started to steer his sled to the side. I knew he wanted me to go first, but there wasn't time. If he slowed down at all, there was no chance.

"Keep going, Nuka!" I yelled as loud as I could. "I'm right behind you!"

Nuka nodded and squatted down as his dogs shot the last narrow strip of ice still connected to the mainland. The dogs made it fine, but the bridge of ice cracked and Nuka's sled runners skimmed over open water. He lost his grip and almost fell off the back, just managing to hang on with one hand.

Seeing open water between myself and the other sleds, I yelled to the dogs and dragged my feet hard in the snow.

"Stop! Kángisârut! Kángisârut!"

The dogs obeyed, but our momentum caused us to get bunched up and we nearly went tumbling into the frigid water. Right away I jumped off the sled and pulled it backward, away from the water.

The channel between me and the mainland was already three or four feet across and widening. Nuka and Gannon stopped their sleds and ran back to the edge of the fracture. Unaaq and Alluaq did the same.

"Oh, man, Wyatt!" Gannon yelled. "This is bad!"

"Yeah, you think?" I shouted.

"Let the dogs try to jump across!" Unaaq yelled. "The ice is moving fast!"

This didn't seem like a good option. We might all fall into the freezing water. Me and six dogs. I wasn't sure how long the dogs would last in that cold, but I knew that if I fell into the water I would only have a minute or two before my heart stopped beating.

"It is the only option!" Unaaq yelled. "Trust in the dogs!"

Trust in the dogs? I still wasn't sure that the dogs even liked me. Would they really risk their own lives to save mine? I needed more time to think.

It was time I didn't have.

"Do it now!" Nuka yelled. "If you wait any longer the crack will be too wide!"

He was right. I climbed on the sled and shouted as I cracked the whip hard over the dogs' heads.

"Go! Huughuaq! Huughuaq!"

The dogs hesitated. I wasn't sure they were going to make the leap. When I shouted again they readied themselves and jumped into the freezing water. The momentum took the lead dogs to the other side of the split where they fought and scratched to pull themselves back onto solid ground. Everyone was there waiting and helped drag them ashore. When the first two dogs were on the other side my sled hit the water, but I didn't have enough momentum to carry the sled across the surface. I honestly thought we were about to sink like a rock.

"Just hang on tight!" Nuka shouted. "The sled should have enough float to carry you across!"

Because I was in such a panic, it hadn't dawned on me that the sleds are made of wood, and wood floats! That gave me hope, but it didn't last. True, wood does float, but a sled is no boat. It could easily tip and even if it didn't topple into the water, the sled wouldn't float for long. Not with all the weight on it.

My boots were submerged to just below the knee, but by then all six dogs were on solid ground and charging ahead with all their might. Everyone grabbed ahold of the sled runners and helped the struggling dogs pull the sled over the lip of the ice to safety.

"Whoa, that was close," Gannon said, and dropped to his knees to catch his breath. "I thought for sure you were Greenlandic shark bait."

Gannon was right. I was almost fish food. At the thought, a hollow feeling washed over me.

"You did good, Wyatt," Unaaq said, probably noticing that I was still stricken with fear. "We're all safe now."

I couldn't speak. Could hardly breathe.

"Wyatt, are you all right?" Nuka asked.

I felt light-headed.

"Earth to Wyatt!" Gannon said. "Come in, Wyatt!"

The mountains in the distance seemed to be moving from side to side. I knew what was happening. I was passing out.

"Yo, Wyatt!" Gannon said. "You okay?"

"I'll be fine," I said. "Just give me a minute."

At that, I crumbled into the snow for an unscheduled nap.

GANNON
LATE NIGHT

Well, after barely avoiding a big-time disaster that almost sent us out to sea on a floating chunk of ice, we were all super-psyched to be back on solid ground. We celebrated in the village with singing and dancing as Alluaq passed out bowls of whale meat that they had left over from their last catch. My lips puckered as I popped one salty chunk after another into my mouth. It was about as rubbery as a bike tire, but surprisingly it didn't taste all that bad.

There's a different kind of excitement that comes with eating a meal when food is so scarce. I mean, at home, eating is something I totally take for granted. When I'm hungry, I just go into the refrigerator, grab whatever looks good, and ten minutes later I'm full. It doesn't work that way in this village. Living in the Arctic, starvation is never far from these villagers' minds. Food here is rationed to make sure it lasts and because that's the case it made me connect with this meal in a way that I never have before. I mean, today I totally savored each and every bite of meat, really tasted it as I chewed, and imagined it nourishing my body after I swallowed it down. Today, maybe for the first time, I appreciated food for what it is—a necessity of life.

Because we didn't return to the village until late, we decided to stay over one more night. Unaaq expects the remainder of this journey to be very challenging and said that a good night's rest is critical. I won't argue with that. I'm totally spent. Nodding off as I write, actually. So, our adventure continues tomorrow, first thing.

WYATT

APRIL 10, 6:14 AM
74° 17' N   56° 11' W
7° FAHRENHEIT, -14° CELSIUS

I woke early this morning and went for a short walk. The rest of the village was still asleep. It was so quiet that the squeak of the snow under my boots seemed loud to the point of being inconsiderate. Not wanting to wake anyone, I sat down on a rock and enjoyed the stark Arctic scenery.

It was only a matter of minutes before I was reminded that you can't sit for long in the Arctic without freezing solid. The cold quickly settled into my bones and I stood to get my blood flowing. Making my way back to the tent, I passed

Alluaq's sled dogs and noticed that one of them was lying on its side, panting heavily. When I knelt at the dog's side, I saw that he had vomited in the snow. His tongue was hanging out of his mouth and his eyes were bloodshot and watery. The dog did not respond to me at all. His condition was serious enough for me to wake Unaaq. Without immediate attention, I thought the dog might die. Unaaq then woke Alluaq and together they went to see what might be done.

"This is Nanook," Alluaq said. "He is one of my youngest dogs, and the one who snapped the shark meat out of my hand yesterday."

"Is that right?" Unaaq said, and went about checking all the other dogs.

The rest of the dogs seemed perfectly healthy and full of energy.

"There might be something wrong with the shark meat," Unaaq said.

"I've never heard of shark making a dog sick," Alluaq said.

Unaaq was deep in thought.

"Many years ago, my grandfather told me a story of a tide that comes to the Arctic once every 100 years," Unaaq said. "This tide carries a harmful bacteria that contaminates the shark meat. After the tide moves away, a full year must pass before the dogs can safely eat the shark meat again."

"Do you believe the tide has come this year?" Alluaq asked.

"It could be so," Unaaq answered.

"Will Nanook die?" I asked.

"I cannot say, but there is a cure."

"What is it?" Alluaq asked.

"I must speak with Papik. He may have what we need to make the remedy."

Unaaq and Alluaq are speaking with Papik now. Hopefully something can be done. As for Gannon and I, it's time to finish packing. We move out soon.

GANNON
APRIL 10

This morning I sat with the poor, sick Nanook, rubbing his thick white coat and trying to comfort him the best I could as Papik and Unaaq whipped up this crazy concoction of fish oils, various animal innards, and the blood of an Arctic hare. Disgusting, I know, but hey, I'm all for whatever might work. Unaaq gave a dose of the gooey brew to the sick dog, Nanook, and asked Alluaq to radio us tomorrow and let us know how he is doing. I'm keeping my fingers crossed.

Thinking that it would be nice to leave the people of the village with something in return for their hospitality, Wyatt and I asked Unaaq and Nuka what sort of gift they might appreciate. Turns out, the women of the village were in need of needles. They had a handful of needles made from bone and could carve more from the shark skeleton, but a good set of steel point needles are more durable and would be very useful, they said. Luckily, we had a few sets that Nuka's mom sent with us to mend tears and stuff, so we offered two full sets to the women of the village and kept one for ourselves. It seemed like such a simple gift, and I worried that it wasn't thanks enough for everything they'd done for us in the way of hospitality. But, that wasn't the case. The needles were a huge hit, and the women of the village showed their thanks with nods of approval and wide smiles and hugs for all of us.

To be honest, I'd love nothing more than to hang out with our new friends for a few more weeks. There are kids here the same age as me and Wyatt, and even though we can't communicate very well, there seems to be a mutual respect between us. I know that in time we could all become the best of friends, one day working together and telling stories and laughing at the same jokes, just a bunch of teenagers, so different and yet so alike. But as Knud Rasmussen wrote, "It is but a short rest, though, that a traveler can permit himself under critical circumstances." Just read that last night in Knud's journals and our mission to save the Inughuit definitely qualifies as "critical circumstances."

WYATT

We're back at it!

We ran approximately 23 miles from the village and stopped for a short break. Clear skies and solid ice so far. Barometric pressure is 29.80 and steady, so this weather should hold for the next day or so. Goal is to cover 70+ miles before the day is out. Another 70+ miles tomorrow.

I'm running well with the dogs and keeping up. Have to get as far as we can while the weather permits. Suunia told us that it's still bad up north and that's where we're headed.

Break time over.

Time to run!

GANNON

LATE AFTERNOON

Okay, heartwarming farewells aside, I ended up leaving the village with a pretty serious pit in my stomach. As I was tying down the last of my gear to the sled, Papik took me and Nuka aside. Apparently he'd just communicated with the spirits, which is totally wild to think about, but even wilder is that these spirits had a message for us. Judging by the way Papik was waving his arms around and squatting down and jumping up into the air and spinning his strips of seal skin like some sort of theater performer, I had a hunch that the spirits' message must have been pretty important.

When he was done, Nuka translated. Basically the message was that we had a dangerous journey ahead. Okay, so that wasn't so much news to me. I mean, come on, we're sledding through Northwestern Greenland. The high Arctic. Of course it's going to be dangerous. But there was one thing in particular Papik said that keeps echoing in my mind like some kind of cryptic warning.

"Beware the blinding light!" he said over and over. "Beware the blinding light!"

WYATT

APRIL 10, 10:22 PM
76° 13' N   55° 48' W
14° FAHRENHEIT, -11° CELSIUS
CLOUDY, WIND 10-15 MPH

Earlier, Unaaq got a radio call from Suunia, who confirmed that the Inughuit sled dogs were fed Greenlandic shark during their hunt. Unaaq believes that must be what made them sick. Before we left the village, he and Papik made as much of the remedy as they could and we brought it with us in a large jug. We're all anxious to hear if the remedy helps Nanook, but we probably won't know until tomorrow.

We have covered 532 miles, which amounts to more than two-thirds of the total distance to the Inughuit. We were given the coordinates of their location, and I calculated that we have approximately 220 miles to go.

Tonight, we're staying in the tent, and the dogs are getting a well-deserved rest. We ran 72 miles today over mostly flat, solid terrain with only a few stretches of uneven ice. All of these miles over a 14 hour period. It was a good, long day of sledding.

I've mentioned that we have had our issues, the dogs and I, but they are good dogs and I am growing more fond of them as the trip goes on. Can't say the feeling is mutual. Not yet, at least. They still snap at me from time to time, but at least they are running well now.

Thanks to the generosity of the villagers, we left with a full chest of seal and whale meat and fed the dogs after our run. They are curled up and sleeping now. Unaaq said they could sleep for days after a long run, getting up only to relieve themselves. But tomorrow we will begin another long day, and they will run without complaint.

Speaking of sleep, I could use some myself.

More tomorrow . . .

Enjoying a well-deserved treat

GANNON

MIDDLE OF THE NIGHT AND I CAN'T SLEEP

Fell asleep for a short stretch and woke having kicked off my blanket. My feet were bare and exposed to the cold air and very nearly the temperature of ice cubes, I'd guess. I put on my thermal socks, which helped warm my feet, but I haven't been able to get back to sleep since. Too much on my mind right now. I can almost hear the thoughts buzzing in my head like a hive of bees. I just can't stop thinking about Papik's warning and wondering what in the world he meant. I'm also thinking about all the great Greenlandic people we've met and their incredible culture and how upsetting it is that their way of life might not be around much longer.

Here's something I read recently: When my parent's were born there were about 6,000 different languages spoken around the world. Now, according to some pretty smart people who study this sort of thing, more than half of those languages aren't spoken anymore. Basically, they've just vanished into thin air. Poof. Most likely gone forever!

Now, here's the problem: Every time we lose one of those languages we also lose thousands of years of knowledge and beliefs and all these different ways of looking at life and the world, which, to me, is like losing a piece of the human spirit.

As travelers, I think we have a responsibility not only to learn from cultures that are different from our own, but to pass on that knowledge. Greenlanders take life as it comes, day to day, and don't ever complain when things get tough. They are taught how to live off the land. They're taught to be resourceful. They are in tune with the environment. Most of us around the world have lost that knowledge, that close bond with nature, and we need to relearn it. It's one of the reasons I spend so much time documenting everything these people teach me. I mean, it isn't unrealistic to think that my journal and video footage might be one of the last records of this ancient culture. Beyond that, I like to think what I learn from others might actually help make me become a better person. Just take the "never complaining" thing as an example. I love that. Imagine living in a society where people don't complain. To never have to hear anyone whine when things don't go exactly their way. I mean, how awesome would that be? You know what, I'm going to try it myself. Lead by example, right?

Okay, time to put away the journal. The cold air has dried my skin to the bone and I've got this pretty nasty crack on my middle finger, which makes it really painful to write, so . . . oh, wait a sec. Am I *already* complaining? Jeez, I guess this is going to be a lot harder than I thought.

WYATT
APRIL 11, 11:03 PM
76° 13' N   55° 48' W
-7° FAHRENHEIT, -22° CELSIUS
CLOUDY, WIND 10-15 MPH

53 miles today. Not as far as we had hoped. Mostly due to a 12 mile stretch of uneven, fractured ice. The surface was so bad we were forced several times to get off our sleds and push them up and over sections of blocky ice that were piled high like fields of boulders. We're approximately 167 miles from the Inughuit people, if my calculations are correct. The goal is to reach them in three days.

The snow conditions where we stopped for the night happened to be ideal for an igloo, and since it's supposed to get much colder tonight we decided building one would be worth the extra effort. It took a total of one hour and twenty minutes to complete. If Gannon and I had been more efficient cutting the blocks out of snow, we probably could have completed it in under an hour.

Here's how it was done:

Using small shovels and saws we cut hard packed snow into square blocks. Unaaq said a good size for the base blocks is about 18 inches high, 24 inches long, and at least 8 inches thick. Fourteen base blocks were placed in a circle, providing just enough space for everyone to fit comfortably inside. Then we stacked another row of blocks on top. Once a block was cut and put into place, the edges were shaved with a blade and smoothed over by hand to bond them together. The trick is to stack the blocks in just the right way to create a dome shaped roof. We constructed the igloo from the inside and when it was finished Unaaq dug a small tunnel about a foot below the base so we could get out. Lastly, we poked small holes into the roof to allow for ventilation when we have a small blubber fire.

In addition to all the small dishes of blubber, Unaaq has a rectangular dish that is about a foot long, which we use for our indoor fires. It probably puts off about as much light and warmth as a dozen candles would, enough to warm the igloo, but not enough to melt the ceiling. There are definitely some drips here and there, but nothing to be concerned with. Unaaq explained that between body heat and a small fire, the temperature inside the igloo can be 40-50°F warmer than it is outside. I thought he must be exaggerating, but after dinner I looked at my thermometer and sure enough, it was

31°F inside the igloo. Compared to the outside temp, it's almost toasty. Then again, a lot of our heat could be coming from Gannon's big mouth.

Note to self: Next time I share an igloo with Gannon, bring earplugs.

GANNON
THE DAY WE DROPPED A NOTCH ON THE FOOD CHAIN!

I'm not lying, I sensed something was wrong right away. Felt it deep down, like a mini-earthquake rumbling in my gut.

All of a sudden, the dogs were acting real jittery and nervous, like something was really bothering them. Then they started making this hissing sound I'd never heard before. That's when I knew for sure that we were in some kind of trouble.

"What's going on?" I said to them. "Is something wrong?"

All of the dogs were facing the same direction, snarling and hissing and real jumpy. Something was out there, hidden in the fog.

But what?

Unaaq and Nuka pulled up next to me and their dogs immediately joined in, hissing and growling. Unaaq knew right away what was bothering the dogs. I could tell by the worried look on his face.

"What is it?" I asked.

"We are being hunted," Unaaq said.

"Excuse me?"

"There is a polar bear nearby," Nuka said.

"Where?" I asked, looking around frantically.

"I do not know exactly," Nuka said, "but the hissing sound the dogs are making tells me that the bear is not far."

"But why would a bear hunt us?"

Unaaq looked at me as if the answer was obvious.

"To eat us," he said.

"Polar bears are the only animal on earth that will hunt the scent of a human," Wyatt said, in his annoying, know-it-all voice.

Okay, I was aware that there are polar bears in the Arctic and it's pretty much common sense that running into one could be problematic. After all, they're giant predators with giant teeth and giant paws and giant appetites. But, what I never knew was that they actually hunt the scent of humans.

"This is a little troubling," I said.

"Do not worry," Unaaq said. "I have a rifle. If the bear comes too close, I will fire off a warning shot. That should be enough to scare it away."

All righty, then. Quick analysis of the facts:

There is a polar bear nearby.

He would like to eat us.

Unaaq has a rifle.

I do not have a rifle.

Unaaq has lots of experience with Polar bears.

I have zero.

So, let's see . . . put two and two and two together and, uh . . . yeah, probably best to stay close to Unaaq.

Real close.

WYATT

APRIL 12, 2:57 PM
77° 04' N   55° 48' W
11° FAHRENHEIT, -12° CELSIUS
CLOUDY, WIND 10-15 MPH

We have traveled 10 miles since the dogs first detected the polar bear. What worries me is that they are still hissing, which means that the bear is following us. That leads me to believe that this is a very hungry bear, and a very hungry bear might not be easy to scare away.

We are surrounded by fog. The visibility cannot be more than 100 feet on all sides, so it is impossible to see where the bear might be.

If we make good distance this afternoon, my hope is that the bear will get tired and give up the chase.

Fog sets in on the ice sheet

GANNON

We built another igloo tonight and my muscles were screaming for mercy, but it's all good because somewhere out there
in all that silence is a polar bear, a bona fide man-eater, quietly stalking us, keeping just enough distance to stay out of
sight, patiently waiting for the right time to pounce, and, let's
be honest, a tent won't stand up very well to a polar bear. At
least an igloo gives us some protection.

Some.

Jeez, the thought of that big bear just gives me the creeps.
I won't lie, I'm afraid to step foot outside. And, to be honest,

I have to go to the bathroom. Bad! But I'll wet my fur pants if I have to because I'm not going anywhere as long as the dogs are hissing. I mean, the bear could be a stone's throw away, hidden in the fog, circling, just waiting for me to walk off alone, thinking to himself, "Oh, man, a nice plate of Gannon tartare would really hit the spot right about now."

Unaaq has his rifle loaded and ready and will be sleeping with it at his side. That should give me some comfort, but for whatever reason, it's just not doing the trick.

WYATT
APRIL 12, 10:34 PM

The polar bear is right outside our igloo! We can hear the bear huffing around, looking for a way inside. The dogs are going wild. Sled dogs are vicious and can put up a fight, so polar bears don't typically mess with them, but if this bear is hungry enough it could take down one or more of the dogs, and that would be a disaster. Just as easily, the bear could push its way inside the igloo and take one of us! Unaaq and Nuka are shouting, trying to scare it away and Unaaq has his rifle cocked, finger on the trigger . . .

GANNON

Unaaq stuck the rifle out the door of the igloo and cracked off two shots—*KA-BOOM! KA-BOOM!* There's a strong smell of gunpowder in the igloo and smoke swirling all around and my ears are ringing like crazy. Unaaq and Nuka told us to stay put and ran outside. It's total chaos right now.

Just heard two more shots fired! Are you kidding me? What's going on out there? Literally, Wyatt and I are about to lose our breakfast we're so scared.

Scared for the safety of the poor dogs! Scared for our lives!

Oh, great Greenlandic spirits, we respect you. Really, we do! Please, please, please protect us!

WYATT
11:56 PM

What a helpless feeling, being trapped in an igloo, knowing that there is an animal outside that is big and fierce enough to eat you.

Everything has settled for the moment and the polar bear is gone. At least, for now. Who knows if it will come back? Unaaq said it ran off after he fired the warning shots into the air. The dogs have calmed down, which makes us feel that it's a good distance away. Fortunately, none of the dogs were harmed when the bear came into camp.

"That was too close for comfort!" Gannon said once we were outside the igloo. "But I have to say, I sure am glad he ran off before Unaaq was forced to add some bear claws to his necklace."

Unaaq chuckled.

"I am glad, too," Unaaq said. "I did not want to hurt the bear. Polar bears are now a threatened species. And this was a big guy. Probably close to 1,500 pounds. Fortunately, he took my warning and moved on. I just hope he will stay away."

In a way, I wish I could have seen the bear, but it ran off before I got outside. I've never actually seen a polar bear and would love to get some photographs of this great predator in its natural habitat. All things considered, though, I should probably just be thankful we all survived the encounter.

GANNON
NIGHTTIME LIGHT SHOW

When I woke, Nuka was standing over me, shaking my arm. It was dark, the middle of the night, but he was fully dressed.

"What's the matter?" I asked, my heart racing. "Is the polar bear back? I knew he'd come back. He's not going to give up until he eats one of us, is he?"

"Just follow me," he said, with a smile. "There's something you must see."

Wyatt was already awake and putting on his jacket, so I did the same and walked outside with Nuka. The air was crisp and immediately went to work, nipping at the exposed skin on my face. Our breath tumbled from our mouths like smoke from a fire. I flipped my hood over my head and buried my nose in the neck of my jacket.

Unaaq was outside, too, his eyes fixed on the sky.

"The Aurora Borealis," Nuka said, sweeping his arm across the horizon.

When I saw the lights, no lie, I almost fell on my butt. I mean, I've never seen anything like it. To be honest, I'm not even sure how to describe it. Really, how does someone capture such magic in words? Maybe if I was a much better writer I could come up with some kind of eloquent wordage that would make people gasp and say, "Oh, that's so beautiful," when they read it, but I'm just not there yet.

I did get some video footage and Wyatt shot at least a million photographs, but this is the kind of phenomenon that video and photos just won't do justice. It's kind of like filming fireworks. The awesomeness of it just doesn't translate to the TV screen. To get the full impact, you have to see it with your own eyes.

Anyway, I guess I should make some kind of attempt at describing the northern lights since we're submitting our field notes to the Youth Exploration Society and all. So, here goes:

What I saw, well, it kind of looked like a bunch of those wispy type clouds lit up in neon greens and reds and caught up in some kind of cosmic wind current. Or like a group of friendly florescent ghosts streaking through the night sky on Halloween. Or like a giant, invisible angel making luminescent brush strokes on a star-speckled canvas. Okay, that might be stretching it a little, but I think it actually describes it pretty well.

Wyatt couldn't help himself and started lecturing us on

the scientific causes of the northern lights, saying things like, "Mmmm, yes, when highly charged electrons cross paths with different elements in the earth's atmosphere, blah-ba-dee-blah-blah-blah, mmm-kay?" Yeah, Wyatt, whatever. All I know is that the Aurora Borealis, without question, is one of nature's most mind-blowing performances!

It's hard to imagine that there is an Arctic storm nearby when we have clear skies and the aurora borealis dancing overhead, but Suunia told us we're about to experience "severe weather," which basically means colder temps, heavy snow, possible white out conditions, and all that other good stuff that comes with a big Arctic storm. We're only a couple days away from the Inughuit, according to Unaaq, which is good news because I think we're all running out of steam.

Okay, then. It's almost time to move out. Frigid fingers crossed that all goes well.

WYATT
APRIL 13, 7:49 PM
0° FAHRENHEIT, -18° CELSIUS
OVERCAST, DARK TO THE NORTH, WIND 10-15 MPH

Today I got my wish. We saw a polar bear!

Gannon spotted him far below on the sea ice, standing motionless over a small hole as streaks of snow and ice blew past him in the wind. Whether it was the bear that was hunting us or not, we do not know.

We took turns looking at the bear through a set of binoculars.

"The Greenlandic people owe a debt of gratitude to this great animal," Unaaq said, speaking loudly to be heard over the wind.

"Why's that?" Gannon asked. "I mean, my memory's not the best, but I'm pretty sure just recently one of them wanted to make a meal out of us."

"Yes," Unaaq said, laughing, "and he would have if we didn't have the gun, but the polar bear is a very wise creature. We learned to hunt, to build proper snow dens, to travel safely on the ice, all by observing the polar bear. Without the guidance of this animal, we would not have been able to survive in the Arctic."

"What's he doing down there?" I asked.

"Seals come up through the holes in the ice to take a breath," Nuka explained. "Polar bears find a hole and wait patiently. When a seal pops its head through the hole, the polar bear eats."

"Better the seal than us, I guess," Gannon said.

"Come now," Nuka said, smacking his mittens together. "We must continue if we want to set up a shelter before the storm reaches us."

We continued for another 11 miles over choppy ice before stopping to build an igloo. The dark gray wall of clouds we've been watching move in from the northwest is nearly upon us. Unaaq has not been able to take his eyes off the approaching storm, which again makes me nervous about what's headed our way.

A polar bear waits to feed

GANNON

Made awesome progress today and are really close to the Inughuit! If the weather doesn't bring us to a halt, it's possible we might even reach them tomorrow and thank goodness for that! They've been trapped for so long my guess is that their dogs are near death and the Inughuit are definitely down to the last of their food, if they have any left at all. Oh, man, we have to reach them soon and I'm talking ASAP, but the final push will really test our stamina and it's important that we get a few hours of rest or exhaustion could put us in even greater danger. So, quick rest and then it's "go time!"

WYATT

APRIL 14, 9:22 AM
77° 42' N   55° 53' W
-4° FAHRENHEIT, -20° CELSIUS
OVERCAST, WIND 15-20 MPH

Getting along decently despite difficult conditions. The cold has settled and we have been taking a steady wind head on. Stopped for a short rest. Taking shelter from the wind behind a high drift.

Hard to believe we were running through standing water and slush only a short time ago. In a week, we have gone from almost summer-like conditions to mid-winter temperatures. The average winter temperature in this part of northern Greenland is -25°F. We're still a ways off that mark, but it is getting colder and the skies have been overcast all day. It's cold enough that the steam from my breath freezes instantly on my face mask. At this point, any exposed skin is susceptible to frostbite, so I am covered head to toe and wearing goggles.

Earlier, we got another radio call from Suunia. She said the weather north of us is intensifying. Another system has moved into the area, creating a powerful atmospheric condition rarely seen. Basically it's an "Arctic superstorm!"

"Be careful out there," Suunia said. "As you know, things can turn dangerous in an instant. I'll make sure to keep you informed on the latest."

When the radio call was over, Unaaq turned to us, his face heavy with concern.

"We have a decision to make," he said. "If we continue north, our risks increase significantly. If we return to the Arctic village, we can take shelter and safely ride out the storm. I could lead you back there and then return north alone."

"We have to keep going!" Gannon blurted out. "I mean, we don't have a choice, do we? The Inughuit are depending on us and we're almost there. If we return to the Arctic village, they'll probably die before you get back to them."

"What do you think, Nuka?" Unaaq asked.

"I agree with Gannon," he said. "Your remedy is their only hope and time is running out. And we're stronger if we stick together as a team. We can help each other."

Unaaq looked to me. I hesitated. Having read the journals of so many polar explorers, I know all too well how these expeditions can end.

"We have enough food to last us a couple weeks," I said. "And adequate gear to keep us warm if we have to take shelter for an extended period." I looked to Unaaq. "If you're confident we can safely ride out the storm in an igloo if it comes to that, then I agree with Gannon and Nuka. We have no choice but to continue. What's your opinion, Unaaq?"

"I agree with each of you," he said. "An igloo will keep

us safe for some time and we have enough food to get us through. I just needed to hear your thoughts before I made my wishes known. We will take every precaution, but I do not want to put any of you at risk if you are unwilling."

"Lead the way, Unaaq," Gannon said. "We're right behind you."

"I applaud your bravery," Unaaq said, bowing his head slightly to us. "Ready your dogs and we will continue north."

At the beginning of this journey, I would have never anticipated we would be in such a difficult situation. Time and again, our resolve has been tested, and yet, we've managed to press on. That is one of the reasons I am optimistic. With Unaaq and Nuka's guidance, I truly believe we can reach the Inughuit.

PART III

THE WRATH OF THE HIGH ARCTIC

Inside the igloo

GANNON

APRIL 15

We are in the belly of the beast! Swallowed whole by the storm! I just hope it doesn't digest us!

As I write, wind and snow are pounding against the igloo, whistling over the rooftop, breaking through narrow seams that have opened in the walls, and whipping snow around inside like a million particles of dust.

When the storm hit Unaaq's suspicions were confirmed—it's a monster! Knowing we didn't have much time, we kicked into high gear, running outside to feed the dogs and tip over the sleds to shelter all of our supplies. Once that was all taken care of, we scrambled back inside the igloo and closed off the entryway for the night.

Right away I grabbed some strips of meat to thaw for dinner and wrapped myself in a big blanket and tried my best to get comfortable. Unaaq is burning a dish of blubber and melting some ice for us to drink and we've got our frozen boots and gloves hanging from hooks above the flames to thaw them out.

Today the dogs' paws got cut up pretty bad on the ice. In serious cold like this the ice can be as sharp as glass. Sometime around mid-day I looked back and noticed bloody prints trailing off behind me in the snow. When we stopped to check their paws, I found that two of my dogs—poor, sweet Najaaraq, and my fastest dog, Anori—had open cuts on the pads of their feet. The other dogs had raw pads, too, and flinched when I ran my finger across them. Unaaq and Nuka assumed we'd run into this type of jagged ice at some point and actually brought a bunch of little hand-stitched booties that slip over the dogs' feet and keep them from being sliced to shreds. These dogs have an incredibly high threshold for pain and would probably run their feet to the bone, but the first order of business on any sled trip is keeping the dogs healthy, so we took the time to fit every one of them with boots. After we put them on and tied them tight around the base of their legs, the dogs whimpered with relief. The benefit of their soft new shoes was obvious, as they ran strong the rest of the day.

It's been such a long day and we're all *dog*-tired. I know, totally lame pun, and it's kind of ridiculous for me to try to hide my feelings with sorry attempts at humor, so I'll just come right out and confess: I'm really scared. It sounds like the Arctic's about to hit us with everything it's got and that's a pretty frightening prospect. I mean, I really don't care to see *everything* the Arctic's got. If we do, it might just be the last thing we ever see!

WYATT

APRIL 15, 10:23 AM
77° 57′ N   52° 14′ W
-12° FAHRENHEIT, -24° CELSIUS
SNOW, 20-30 MPH WINDS

As bad as this storm is, we are safe inside a sturdy igloo. When we checked on the dogs they were all curled up and sleeping. Most of them are completely buried in the snow, only their noses showing. Unaaq explained that the snow actually insulates them from the cold and assured us they are comfortable. I wish I could say the same for myself. My thermometer inside the igloo reads 30°F. It is even warmer under my blanket, but I have a nagging chill that I cannot shake.

We radioed Suunia for the extended forecast. Unfortunately, it is not promising. The blizzard shows no signs of letting up. In weather like this, Unaaq says it would be a challenge to go a single mile in a day, and storms up here can last a long time. We are all so anxious to get to the Inughuit and we're very close. However, we have no choice but to stay hunkered down in the igloo until conditions improve.

GANNON

The weather settled just enough for us to pack up and make a short run on the sleds. That's not to say the weather is good. Not even close. It's still snowing like crazy and the wind is charging over the ice, building up snowdrifts so high the dogs are having a hard time getting through them.

I have to admit, I've been tempted at times to exaggerate my bravery in this journal so that one day I could look back and say, "Wow, G-Man. You were one tough hombre!" Right now, though, I can't even pretend to be tough. Honest truth, I'm on the verge of weeping like a baby.

What hurts most is the bitter cold. Running the sled, the pain always starts in my fingertips and toes and then moves inward until both of my hands and feet are aching like they're being crushed by some invisible force. When I took off my face mask to break away the ice that had formed around the mouth, my skin started to sting like someone was holding a match to it. Within a matter of minutes it was so numb that my face muscles stopped functioning properly and I literally couldn't speak without slurring my words. I'm not even sure what the temperature is, but it's cold enough to freeze spit mid-air! I'm not kidding, before it hits the ground! Now, that's *frostbite* cold!

My muscles are cramping and I have all these open cuts on my hands that just won't heal. Worst of all, I've developed this strange sounding cough. Kind of like a hyena might sound after a tonsillectomy. And it burns, which I know is not a good thing.

That's right, I'm complaining again. Sorry, but given our situation, I really don't have much of an option.

We've stopped again and dug out a small cave in a snow-drift to block the wind and are boiling noodles. Not sure how much further we'll get today.

WYATT

APRIL 15, 2:19 PM
78° 14' N   51° 09' W
-11° FAHRENHEIT, -24° CELSIUS
ELEVATION: 7,371 FEET
BLIZZARD CONDITIONS

If my calculations are correct, we're just over 20 miles from the Inughuit.

Other than that, I'm afraid we have no real positive news to report. My left foot is starting to go numb. Both hands, as well. Gannon has a serious cough and a burning in his chest. Could be a sign of bronchitis, or worse. He started taking anti-biotics as a precaution. I think Unaaq and Nuka are struggling, too. Both are moving slower and Nuka has the beginnings of a cough, but neither has made a single complaint.

Just as Unaaq feared, we are in the grips of a super storm. Can't even get a radio call though to Suunia. The storm must be blocking the transmission.

Our progress has slowed to a pace of about 2-3 mph. Hard to do much better than that in 30-40 mph winds. Despite these challenges, we must continue to move on the best we can. We must move to keep the blood flowing and get closer to the Inughuit.

Worthy of note is Unaaq's good nature, which remains in tact. I don't think I've ever met a more compassionate and caring man. When we stop to rest, he tends to us first and regularly makes jokes to lift our spirits. Here's one that got a laugh from all of us:

"Once, three friends got together at the tavern in northern Greenland," Unaaq began. "Naturally, their conversation turned to how cold it was outside and how uncomfortable their igloos were. All three claimed theirs was the coldest, so they decided to go check out each and see who, in fact, had the coldest igloo.

"They went to the first man's house and he said, 'Check this out!' and poured out a glass of water, which froze solid before it hit the ground.

"'That's cold,' said the second man, 'but my igloo is colder.' They went to the second man's igloo and he said, 'Wait until you see this!' and exhaled a deep breath which froze solid in the air and fell to the ground in an icy clump.

"'Wow,' said the third man. 'That is cold, but my igloo is even colder.'

"So they went to the third man's igloo and watched as he pulled back his blanket and picked up a single ball of ice.

"'What is that?' one of the other men asked.

"'I will show you,' he said, and lit a match under the ice. "'Listen closely.' As it warmed to just the right temperature the ice went, 'Faaaaaaart!'"

Maybe we're a bit delirious, but we all laughed like it was the funniest thing we'd ever heard.

"Is that a joke that was passed down from your ancestors?" Gannon asked.

"No," Unaaq said, still laughing. "My brother found it on the internet."

That made us all laugh even harder. Gannon's eyes were watering.

"Oh, jeez," Gannon said, "The tears are freezing to my cheeks."

"I'm sorry," Unaaq continued, "I know it is immature to tell such a joke, but a wise man once said, laughter is the best medicine."

So true.

GANNON

Oh, man, we just can't catch a break. I mean, come on, Mother Nature! Enough already, okay? Hello? Can you hear me?

Ah, she's not listening.

Unaaq says the Inughuit people are not far, but when the weather overpowers us like it's doing right now, we have no choice but to take shelter and get a small fire going to thaw our hands and feet and face and warm some frozen meat to eat. Facing this weather on a sled is harder than I could have ever imagined. We never experienced anything even close to this when we trained in Colorado. If we stop moving while we're outside, even for a minute, our clothes stiffen and become hard as cement. I have to warm my pen over the blubber lamp for a good ten minutes to thaw the ink before I can even write in my journal. Our supply cases freeze like they've been sealed with a padlock. Even with my goggles on, the humidity from my breath worked its way inside and froze my right eye shut during the last run, which was just crazy. I had to steer the dogs with one eye until I couldn't take the pain and asked Unaaq to stop so we could melt the ice away.

Walls of an ice cave

Not to be a downer or anything, but all the beauty of the Arctic disappears in weather like this. The cold is just vicious, attacking with relentless force. I now understand why so many explorers called this place "inhospitable." No beating around the bush, this is the kind of weather that puts explorers in an icy grave.

The wind has died down some since I started writing and Unaaq went out to check the conditions. If he gives us the thumbs up, we'll try to log some extra miles. Really not sure where I'm going to find the strength, but I have to be ready, just in case.

Okay, Unaaq came back and we all agreed to cover as much distance as we can before nightfall.

Well, here we go . . .

WYATT

APRIL 15, 11:23 PM
78° 31′ N   53° 58′ W
-14° FAHRENHEIT, -26° CELSIUS
BLIZZARD CONDITIONS

We were in a white out when I lost sight of everyone. I shouted their names. Again and again, I shouted. There was no response. None that I could hear over the screaming wind, at least. It's likely they were no more than ten feet away, but there was zero visibility.

I was trying to clear the snow from my goggles when the dogs made a sharp left. Suddenly, I felt the sled leaning hard to one side. It was being pulled, tipping over. Quickly, I leaned in the opposite direction, but it was too late. As the sled toppled over, I instinctively locked my arms around the wooden handrails, knowing that if the dogs ran off without me I wouldn't have a chance. There was a crash and everything came to a jolting halt. Several pieces of important gear were jarred loose and I found myself hanging on for dear life. On either side of me were sheer cliffs of ice. Nervously, I looked down. Below my feet, the blue ice faded into a dark abyss. I was hanging over a massive crevasse.

I could feel the dogs tugging at the sled, trying to pull it out of the crevasse, but it was no use. Judging by the width of the crevasse, I knew the sled was too wide to fall any deeper. It was wedged securely. If I were to lose my grip, though, I'd fall beneath the ice. There would be no way to climb out. I'd be stuck in the crevasse and freeze to death. That would be it. The end of everything.

I needed to get myself out of the crevasse. Snow was swirling in my face as I struggled to hold on. With my feet, I pushed against one side of the ice, pressing my back onto the other side. Bracing myself with my legs, and keeping one arm on the sled, I moved slowly up the ice, eventually making my way to the top of the crevasse where I pulled myself back into the raging storm.

I was out of breath and could have rolled over and passed out from exhaustion, but fear kept me going. I jumped to my feet and shouted at the top of my lungs for help.

"Gannon! Unaaq! Nuka!"

When I turned into the wind, my goggles were immediately plastered with snow. I wiped them clean, but even then I could not see more than a foot in front of my face. I reached out with my hands and found the edge of a sled runner. Holding the runner tightly, I knelt back down. I could not risk making a wrong step and falling back into the crevasse. Inching forward on my hands and knees I found the dogs and checked each of them for injury. They were all safe, and once I had them settled down they curled up in the snow and buried their noses under their tails.

Remembering what Unaaq and Nuka had taught us, I knew I had to build a shelter and quick. Carefully, I crawled back to the crevasse and was relieved to find my backpack with the snow shovel still strapped to the sled. Bracing myself so I wouldn't fall into the crevasse, I reached underneath and loosened the strap, taking great care not to drop the backpack. Once I had it securely in hand, I removed the shovel and began clearing a hole in a drift. When I was done digging a small cave, I crawled back outside and yelled into the wind once more.

"Gannon! Unaaq! Nuka!"

I may as well be on another planet.

No one can hear me.

No one is going to find me.

I am on my own.

The snow cave will keep me safe for now, but I don't have

much in my backpack. Only my journal, a map, matches, a couple weather gauges, and three small dishes of seal fat, one of which I am already burning for warmth. The radio was in another bag and I don't know if it fell into the crevasse or not, but I was not able to find it. When the storm settles enough, I will see if any other equipment can be salvaged.

GANNON
TAKING SHELTER INSIDE CAVE

This is bad! Seriously, it's worse than bad! I'm trying so hard to hold it together, but Wyatt is lost out there in this Arctic blizzard and I'm just freaking out!

One minute he's right behind us and then out of nowhere this gale hits us dead in the face and the visibility goes to nothing and next thing I know he's gone, swept away by the storm. I would've been lost, too, if Unaaq and Nuka hadn't pulled along side of me and tied our sleds together with a rope. Now we're holed up in a cave Unaaq found in a rock ledge, and thank goodness for that, because I'm not sure how much longer we would have survived out there.

Wyatt's not responding to any of our radio calls, which makes me want to charge back into the storm and find him, but that's just too dangerous. Basically, I have no choice but to wait until the storm dies down, and the waiting part is the absolute worst torture I can imagine!

Staring through this narrow opening in the cave wall and

seeing all that white flying by out there, it's like some kind of evil spirit has unleashed his wrath upon us. Now I understand what Papik meant when he said, "Beware the blinding light."

This storm, it's the *blinding light*!

WYATT
APRIL 16, 9:44 AM
-19° FAHRENHEIT, -28° CELSIUS
FOGGY, LIGHT SNOW, 15-25 MPH WINDS

The storm let up just enough to inspect my sled. As I suspected, it is badly damaged, wedged and frozen into the crevasse. The left runner is split in two places. Without tools and new wood for repair, the sled is of no use. I was able to retrieve one blanket. It was still tied to the deck. Everything else fell into the crevasse. Most critical, my radio and food supply. There is no food for the dogs either. Our only hope is rescue.

GANNON
STILL INSIDE CAVE
DON'T KNOW THE DATE ANYMORE

Unaaq took my sled and set out into the storm alone to try to find Wyatt. Even though I begged and pleaded, he wouldn't let me go with him. Some of my fingers and the tip of my nose are practically frostbitten so Unaaq insisted I stay with Nuka and make a run for the Inughuit as soon as the snow lets up.

When Unaaq was getting ready to leave, he gave us the coordinates of the Inughuit and told us how to administer the remedy to the dogs.

"Give each dog two spoonfuls," he said. "Use the handle of your whip to keep their mouths open so they don't bite down on your hand. Stick the remedy deep into their mouths, near the back of their tongue. That way they are forced to swallow it."

Nuka and I both nodded, but I was a total wreck and desperately needed some kind of reassurance. I needed to hear Unaaq tell me not to worry, that everything would be okay, that he would definitely be able to find Wyatt. Being the great leader that he is, Unaaq gave me that reassurance.

"Wyatt is a smart boy and knows what to do," Unaaq said. "He will build a shelter and stay there so that I can find him. We will meet up again very soon, and once we're all safely in Siorapaluk we will have a great celebration."

Oh, man, I hope so.

Before he left, we all hugged.

"Make sure to save some food for me and Wyatt," Unaaq said with a smile. "I think we will have worked up quite an appetite by the time we get there."

"We'll save you all the best strips of jerky," Nuka said.

Unaaq chuckled and pulled his hood over his head. Calmly, he turned and walked from the cave, vanishing like a ghost into the driving snow.

WYATT

APRIL 16, 11:56 AM
-21° FAHRENHEIT, -29° CELSIUS
BLOWING SNOW, 20 MPH WINDS, GUSTS TO 30 MPH

I stuck a long metal pole into the ground and am flying the Youth Exploration Society flag that I brought to plant at the northern most point of our journey. Though visibility is no more than 15 feet, I'm hoping that they will see it. A hard cold is coming from the north and the storm shows no sign of letting up.

I dug my cave approximately two feet deeper, putting more distance between myself and the storm. I cannot dig any further, as I've hit a wall of ice. Now I must keep my blood flowing to prevent frostbite. When my extremities go numb, I stomp my feet on the ground and smack my hands against my chest until the feeling comes back.

My thoughts continue to drift to my parents, my brother, my home. So much on my mind, but that is all I can write for now.

GANNON

INUGHUIT IGLOO CAMP

Okay, I have no idea how he did it. Maybe the dogs sniffed this place out somehow, but whatever the case, I have to give Nuka a huge amount of credit. He's like some kind of teenage superhero the way he found the Inughuit in this crazy storm.

The agony of being out in that blizzard, taking that hurricane force wind dead in the face, it's pretty much impossible to put it into words. We couldn't see more than ten feet ahead of us the whole way, and we got here just in time. Another hour or so in that cold and we would have lost a few body parts to frostbite.

Some of the Inughuit came out of their igloos to greet us when they heard the dogs. They were smiling and definitely happy to see us, but the snow was blowing hard and few words were spoken as they helped us tie down the dogs and remove our gear from the sleds. We dragged our stock of food into the igloo and made hot tea and handed out a ration of jerky and biscuits to everyone.

There are fourteen Inughuit people here. A few women and a couple of boys around my age. The rest are men. My guess is that our food can last three days if we do a good job rationing. The remedy Unaaq made for the dogs is frozen solid and we're trying to warm it enough so that we can give each of the dogs a dose. The sooner we can do that the better, because we need to leave for Siorapaluk before we're out of food. If the dogs don't improve, we'll make a run with Nuka's dogs, but our sled will only hold a few people, at most. So even if we're able to make it all the way there, we'll have to come back with lots of help to get everyone else out. No matter what happens, restoring the health of these dogs is critical. If the remedy doesn't work, a lot of us will starve.

After being stranded here for so long, the poor Inughuit

are in worse shape than we are. They ran out of food days ago and it shows in their faces. Most have sunken cheeks and dark eyes that hold distant, blank stares. And their movements are real slow. I think these long Arctic storms have a crazy numbing effect on a person's brain. I mean, you push yourself to the limit in this kind of weather, but ultimately something's got to give. At times, I've felt like I had exhausted just about the last of my energy. My mind would get stuck in slow motion and my body became this empty, lifeless shell. I'd sit there in a near stupor and wonder how I was managing to keep from falling over dead. I'm actually feeling another wave of exhaustion come over me now. I sure hope this food helps restore some of our strength.

But, honestly, I'm not worried about us right now. At least we're sheltered from the storm. What I'm worried about is Wyatt and Unaaq.

WYATT

APRIL 17, 1:51 PM
-23° FAHRENHEIT, -31° CELSIUS
BLIZZARD CONDITIONS, 50+ MPH WINDS

My entire body is stiffening. So numb, even the slightest movements take thought and effort. My lips are cracked and bleeding. My tongue is like a dried sardine. The taste in my mouth is almost nauseating. What I wouldn't pay for a heater, toothbrush, and some lip balm right about now.

All but one dish of seal fat has been burned. What I have remaining will be used within the day. I continue to move my fingers and toes to keep circulation flowing and I ate some snow earlier, but what I'm craving most is food. If I had something to eat, I would not be as concerned for my safety.

To pass the time I have thought a lot about what I will do when I get home. First order of business, I've decided, will be to get a big juicy cheeseburger and a mountain of fries from Woody Creek Tavern, my favorite burger restaurant. Then, I think I'll wash the burger and fries down with a mammoth pepperoni slice from New York Pizza, one of the best pizza joints in the whole world. At the moment, I am having visions of food that are so vivid I can practically smell it. Oh, if only these visions could fill my empty stomach.

GANNON

Warmed the remedy to an icy slush and gave all 36 dogs two spoonfuls, just like Unaaq instructed. Dogs are lethargic. Sick and probably close to starvation. Hoping they'll bounce back somehow. Plan to give them another dose tomorrow and try to feed them. We'll know a lot more then.

WYATT
APRIL 17, 10:03 PM
-24° FAHRENHEIT, -31° CELSIUS
BLIZZARD CONDITIONS

Barometric pressure at 30.10 millibars and steady. Wind blowing from the WNW, bringing cold from the top of the world. This storm does not seem to be going anywhere.

A numbness has settled in the toes of my left foot and I'm also losing feeling in my left hand. Frostbite, I'm afraid. Could use sleep, but my concern is that I will not wake up. Again, my hope is that a rescue is underway.

GANNON

Not even time functions properly in this cold. It's slowed to a halt, just like everything else. Each minute feels like an eternity. I honestly don't know how long we've been on this ice sheet anymore. I've totally lost track. Days, weeks, months? Doesn't matter, I guess.

I wish there was a way for me to reach my parents. It would be so nice to hear their voices. Then again, I dread having to pass along this news. I dread it more and more with each passing minute. No joke, I feel like I'm going insane.

Hold it together, I keep telling myself over and over.

Hold it together, Gannon.

Hold it together!

Oh, man, if I could trade places with Wyatt I'd do it in a second flat. No questions asked. I'd do anything to save him. Anything!

WYATT

APRIL 18, 9:51 AM

Got good news and bad news.

Good news first. I have stopped shivering and am comfortable, strangely enough. The bad news, this means hypothermia has entered its final stage. In other words, I am dying, freezing to death right where I sit. Never thought I would write such a thing, but it is a fact. My seal blubber is gone. Without fire it is hard to generate warmth. Especially at -25°F.

I keep dreaming about what other kids around the world might be doing right now. Swimming or biking or just hanging out with friends. Maybe eating a hot meal or sleeping in a warm bed. How I wish I were doing one of those things. How I wish things had turned out differently. Whether it's a couple days or a matter of hours, the time I have left is short.

GANNON

Where are you, brother? Has Unaaq found you? Are you both making your way here? Bravely battling the storm? Trying with all you've got to save yourselves? I am sending you all my energy. I hope you can feel it. I hope it helps you find your way back to us. Please, Wyatt, find your way.

WYATT

1:24 PM

My eyes opened at the sound of crunching snow. I thought I was having some kind of hallucination, or that maybe I had died, because there before me, crawling out of the storm, was Unaaq. His face was a solid sheet of ice, almost unrecognizable. Icicles dangled from his beard, his furs were plastered with snow, his eyelids almost frozen shut.

How could this be?

How had he found me?

Unaaq collapsed at my feet and I dragged him further inside, out of the wind. He could barely speak.

"Unaaq," I said, "Can you hear me? Are you okay?"

"I have supplies," he said in a slurred, whisper of a voice. "And a radio."

I tried to brush the ice away from his face, but it was frozen to his skin. I needed to warm the cave. Warm Unaaq.

Adrenaline took over. My heart was racing. Life was once again flowing through me. There was no choice. I had to go back into the storm and bring Unaaq's supplies back to the cave. Outside, it was blinding. I couldn't see anything. Fortunately, the dogs were all barking. I followed the sound to the sled, untied several containers and began dragging them back through the deep snow, but the wind was blowing so hard I couldn't find the cave. There was absolutely no visibility. I tried to shield my eyes from the wind, but I still couldn't see a thing.

I would freeze to death if I didn't find my way back to the cave. I knew this and became frantic, moving around in circles, searching desperately for the entrance. Finally, I stumbled upon the flag I had planted outside the cave. Scrambling back inside, I wrapped us both in fur blankets and hung another blanket over the shovel at the entrance to block the wind. My left hand had almost no feeling, which made it difficult to manage the blubber lamps. Finally, I got one lit and then a second. The cave filled with smoke and the smell of charred seal fat. I waved it out the best I could.

The heat from the lamps might possibly be the greatest thing I have ever felt. I am thawing out my hands, wiggling and clapping them over the flame. The cave has warmed considerably. I am keeping the flames close to Unaaq in an effort to melt the ice away from his face.

No luck yet with the radio. I tried to reach Gannon, Nuka, or anyone from Siorapaluk, but I'm getting only static. Also sent an SOS in the hopes someone out there receives it.

GANNON

We gave the dogs a second dose of medicine and mixed in a couple chunks of seal meat to get some protein in their system. I may have been imagining this, but it seemed like they had a little more pep this morning. Now, again, we must wait to see if they improve.

Inside the big igloos, we mostly pass the time in silence. Everyone is tired and cold and hungry. We're all wrapped in blankets. Sleeping on and off. Occasionally, someone will speak and Nuka will translate. They tell stories of the Arctic and how the weather has changed in their lifetime. How it is no longer predictable. How the seasons are confused. Warmer in the winter, less ice, more open water, then an unusual blizzard like this one so late in the season. So much of their life is dictated by the weather and everything is changing, they say.

Looking around at all the faces of the Inughuit, I am in awe. It would be impossible for me to feel anything but respect for them. It's just mind-blowing that for thousands of years they have been able to exist up here in this unforgiving climate. As we sit here, trapped in this terrible storm, it just doesn't seem possible that anything could survive.

WYATT

APRIL 19, 7:36 AM
-22° FAHRENHEIT, -30° CELSIUS
HEAVY SNOW AGAIN, WINDS 30+ MPH

Unfortunately, Unaaq is in bad shape. The ice on his face melted away, revealing serious damage. His eyes are terribly swollen and several large blood blisters have developed on his nose and cheeks. He doesn't even look like himself. I am warming us up the best I can, but it will take a while, as I'm only burning one blubber dish at a time to keep from using it all up too quickly.

I opened one of his supply containers and found some meat and a half dozen biscuits, enough to keep us going for a few days, dogs included. Unable to wait long enough to thaw the meat, I dropped a frozen strip in my mouth and let it sit there, savoring the salty flavor as the ice melted away. I could almost feel my body absorbing the nutrients. Then I crawled into the gale and gave a handful of meat to each of the dogs. Unaaq will need to eat soon, too. He will never be able to travel by sled unless he gets his strength back. Judging by his condition, he has been out in the storm since we separated. He risked his life to save mine. Now I must return the favor.

I still cannot get through to anyone on the radio. It may be no use. Worse, the battery is nearly dead.

No one can hear us.

No one can get to us.

GANNON

Knud Rasmussen wrote that northern Greenland is "a land without heart where everything living must fight a hard battle for life and food." I keep wondering what he would do in this situation. In all those years he explored the Arctic,

Knud experienced just about every kind of hardship imaginable. Unfortunately, things didn't always go as planned and sometimes they actually went a lot worse than planned, like during the Second Thule Expedition. The weather got so bad even Knud's crew couldn't avoid tragedy. Two of the men on that expedition died, and we're talking about some of the most experienced polar explorers there ever were. I'm sorry, but we have to face reality. We're not immune to tragedy. Sometimes we might think we are, but that's just ignorance. Truth is, lots of explorers far stronger and more experienced than us have died, and if it happened to them, it could definitely happen to us.

WYATT

10:08 PM
-27° FAHRENHEIT, -33° CELSIUS

Unaaq woke earlier and was able to take a few sips of water. He could not eat, though. Had no appetite. Amazingly, he still manages a smile when he speaks.

"What is the condition of your sled?" he asked, his voice cracking in the cold.

"It's stuck in a crevasse and badly damaged," I said. "Without major repairs, it's useless."

"Have you checked the dogs?" he asked.

"Yes," I said. "I fed them earlier and they seem to be holding out okay."

"If the weather breaks you must take the good sled. Do not worry about me."

"I won't leave you, Unaaq. We'll get out of this together."

"You will know when it is time to make a run and at that time, you must go. I am too far along to travel. I would only slow you down and put us both in danger. You must be able to run the sled fast and freely if you hope to make it."

"I could never leave without you," I said. "I'm sorry, I just couldn't do it."

"I am an old man," he said, and was consumed by a hacking cough. I gave him another sip of the snow I had melted. When his cough settled, he continued with a smile. "Should it be my fate, I am ready to begin my journey in the next life."

"Please don't talk like that, Unaaq. We're going to get out of this together."

"There is no need to fear death. It is part of our experience. Every one of us."

I turned my head away and fought back tears.

"This conversation is not meant to be sad," he continued. "I do not see it that way, and I do not want you to see it that way either."

He smiled at me and closed his eyes. Soon, he was asleep.

Unaaq selflessly came back for me and together we will fight this out to the bitter end.

I will not leave him.

I will not let him die.

GANNON

Finally, something has gone our way! The dogs seem to be coming around! I mean, it's pretty much a miracle, but it looks like Unaaq's remedy is really doing the trick! Several of them are back on their feet, moving around, howling, showing real signs of life.

Nuka and some of the Inughuit are outside tending to them now. They need more food in them if they're going to pull everyone to Siorapaluk. As of now, the plan is to leave tomorrow morning, no matter what the weather. I am not looking forward to going back out there, but we really have no choice.

I'm hoping that Wyatt and Unaaq make their way here before we leave. I mean, they have to. I can't imagine leaving without them. If it comes to that, oh man, I honestly don't know what I'll do.

WYATT
APRIL 20, 1:53 PM

When Unaaq woke, he looked me straight in the eyes. A smile came over his face and he lay there for some time, quiet and thinking.

Finally, he made an effort to sit up and I helped him.

"Are you feeling better?" I asked.

"I will be okay," he said, though his voice did not indicate that he was any better. In fact, it was so faint, it seemed the voice of a ghost.

"I have a story to tell you," Unaaq said. "It is a story my father told me many times when I was a boy."

I moved closer to him so I could hear.

"Once there were two caribou, a father and a son, and they were making a long trek over the ice. The father was a wise, old caribou. But as it happens, a polar bear picked up their scent and began trailing them. And though the polar bear was careful to stay out of sight, the father caribou knew that it was near. He stopped his son and spoke to him.

"'Son,' he said, 'you must continue towards the coast where your mother will be waiting. Take her further still to the place where the snow melts away and the grasses grow in the summer. There is something that I must do alone.'

"'Will you meet us in the grasslands, father?'

"The father looked at his child and said, 'We will all be joined again when the time comes.'

"The child was afraid to go without his father. He worried that he might never see him again. However, his instincts told him that his father's wisdom should not to be questioned. 'Yes, father,' said the young Caribou, and continued on.

"The father knew that if he did not face the polar bear alone, it would take them both. His son was still young and had a long life to live. There were many things the young caribou had not yet experienced. His father would not allow his life to end so soon. Once the son was far enough away, the elder caribou went to face the polar bear.

"The bear said to the caribou, 'Where is your son?'

"'He has gone ahead.'

"'Then I must chase him.'

"'He is already far from here.'

"'Then I will run fast and catch him.'

"'It is possible. However, if you do, you will lose out on me and I am almost three times his size. Whom would you rather have?'

"The next day the son reached his mother and they went south to the place where the snow melts away and the grass grows in the summer. In time, the son began to understand the wisdom the father had passed on to him as a child and eventually he grew into a great leader."

Unaaq's story consumed me. While he told it I almost forgot the grave situation we faced ourselves.

"Excuse me, Wyatt," Unaaq said. "I must step outside. I need some time to myself."

With great effort, Unaaq lifted himself and crawled forward, disappearing into the storm. I have gone out twice to look for him, but he is nowhere to be found. The second time out I tethered all of the dogs to one sled just in case the storm lets up enough to make a run. This task drained all but the very last of my energy. I am desperate to help Unaaq, but my body is shutting down. If I go out again, I'm afraid I won't make it back.

Being stuck here, with all this time to think, I've realized that there are a lot of things I wish I had said to certain people when I had the chance. I'm beginning to think I should put some of these things down in my journal. Some thoughts for Mom, Dad, and Gannon.

"A Letter to My Family"
Written on April 20, day #20 of our expedition

Dear Mom, Dad, and Gannon,

This is a letter I never expected to write. Though, I guess I am fortunate to have the strength to do it. Unaaq has walked off into the blizzard so that I might have a chance to live. Together we would have no hope of making it to safety. Fact is, he was too far gone. We both knew this. His concern for me must be recorded. Please pass along to Nuka and the rest of his family that he was the wisest, most compassionate, and bravest man I ever had the pleasure of knowing. Surely, they will understand this, but I hope it will provide some comfort to hear that these characteristics remained with him until the very end.

Despite Unaaq's brave act, I'm afraid I am unable to continue. Since being stranded, my hopes have been placed on a change in the weather. Unfortunately, the only change was from bad to worse. Outside the temperature is -20°F, with a wind chill so fierce I have no desire to calculate it. I have enough food to keep from starving, a box of tea to drink, and for the most part I am comfortable. There is simply nothing more that can be done against this cold. It is overtaking me. I see signs of worsening frostbite on my left foot and hand, though the pain is not as bad as you might think. The exhaustion is the toughest part. It takes a tremendous effort just to get these words down.

I remember everything about you. I can see you all almost as clearly as if you were sitting in front of me. It is a comfort to think of you. To play all the memories in my mind. There are too many to mention, but each one has brought a smile to my face. I just wish I could reach out and hug all of you one last time. I am trying to put on a brave face in this letter, but the fact of the matter is that I am terrified of the end.

It will probably be said that we pushed it too far. We may have, but it was done in an attempt to save the lives of others. What better reason is there to risk your own? We made a great attempt to help the Inughuit, and my hope is that Gannon and Nuka were able to complete our mission. My situation is the result of an accident. If anyone is at fault, it is me. No one else.

I do hope this unfortunate incident does not diminish your love of travel and exploration. I would be forever upset if I knew that was the outcome. Sometimes in exploration there are factors well beyond anyone's control. It has been made clear to me how fragile a species we really are in the face of Mother Nature's extremes. That being said, I would not change a thing we have done. When you pursue big dreams, you must accept big risks. I hope that all of you will continue down this path. There are still so many places to see and lots of good that can be done. Know that I will be with

you in spirit wherever you go. I love you all
more than you can imagine. You have made my
life one great adventure and for that I feel
blessed. Please remember me and continue in
our effort, no matter how small it may be,
to help make the world a better place. On
that end, please pass along my journal and
scientific records to the Youth Exploration
Society. I hope they will be useful.

Lastly, to Gannon, my brother and best
friend. I do hope that this letter finds
you safe and warm along with Nuka and the
Inughuit people we tried so desperately to
reach. Thanks for all the laughs. I don't
know that I would have ever developed a
passion for exploration had it not been for
your free-spirited ways.

Until next time,
your loving son and brother,

Wyatt

GANNON

It all happened like a real-life horror film playing out before
my eyes. The sky was this dark and sinister shade of gray. A
light rain was falling. It was just me and my mom and dad
walking up this gently sloping hill, our boots crunching over
the last of the spring ice. We aren't saying a word to each
other, just moving up the slope, dreading each step as we
come closer and closer to a little white cross sitting alone
on the top of the hill. Then all of a sudden it's like I'm being

pulled forward in fast-motion. Moving effortlessly over the ground to a rectangle of freshly shoveled dirt at the base of the cross. There, on the cross, I see an inscription that rocks me like a bolt of lightening:

The grave, it's Wyatt's!

Suddenly, every cell in my body detonates and I literally jump out of my blanket. I'm dazed and confused and feel the tears in my eyes. Then, finally it dawns on me—I'm inside the igloo!

Everyone is staring at me. Nuka sits up and asks if I'm okay. I take a deep breath and tell Nuka that I'm fine, but really, I'm about as far from fine as I could be. Outside the storm rages on, the wind whistling like some kind of haunting Arctic symphony. My fear is that the dream was real, like some kind of premonition being communicated to me by the spirits or something. I'm terrified that my brother is gone!

WYATT
APRIL 20, 11:57 PM

Storm and winds have diminished some, but I am too weak to take readings. It seems appropriate that I say farewell to the dogs. We had our troubles early on, but they proved loyal and saved us several times on this long sled journey. I will release them and hope they find their way to safety. It will most likely take everything I have to complete this task. It's difficult to admit such a truth, but I'm afraid this will be my last entry.

GANNON

First there was a howl, then another. Then, just like that, all the dogs were barking like mad. I figured they were warning us of some kind of danger, probably another polar bear or something, but after listening closely I realized these barks were different than the sound we'd heard them make when the polar bear was nearby.

Nuka and I and a few of the Inughuit men stepped outside and made our way to the dogs.

"What is it?" Nuka said to the dogs. "Huh? What's going on?"

The dogs kept howling and barking and pulling at their leashes like they were desperate to take off in a full sprint. I turned around and looked into the fog. I still couldn't see anything, but in the distance—way, way off—was a muffled sound. It kept getting louder and louder until it was unmistakable. It was the sound of dogs. Other dogs. Somewhere out of sight, dogs were running!

"Do you hear that?" I asked Nuka.

"Yes," he said. "Sled dogs."

We were both thinking the same thing, but were afraid to say it. We didn't want to build up our hopes that by some miracle Unaaq and Wyatt were alive, only to have them crushed.

Nuka and I walked further away from the igloos, anxious

for something to materialize in the frozen Arctic haze. The anticipation was killing me and the barking kept getting louder and then finally an image appeared, faint at first, then clear enough to see. Right there before our eyes a pack of sled dogs emerged from the fog like a group of phantoms. I counted twelve dogs total, all tied to a single wooden sled. It was one of our sleds!

But the sled was empty. No one was driving it. My stomach was in my throat as Nuka and I ran out on the ice and stopped the dogs. On the sled was a pile of fur blankets tied down with ropes. Nothing else. Where in the world were Wyatt and Unaaq? What had happened to them?

We unraveled the ropes and tore the blankets away one by one. That's when we made an unbelievable discovery. Curled up and unconscious on the sled was my brother!

Right away I ripped off my gloves and found my way under his coat, checking his neck for a pulse. It was hardly detectable, a beat every few seconds, maybe. He was in pretty bad shape, just about frozen solid with these dark, sunken eyes and red blisters all over his face, but I was out of my mind with excitement. He was alive!

Unaaq had taken my sled to find Wyatt. Kamik and the rest of my dogs were harnessed to the sled right along side Wyatt's dogs, but Unaaq was missing. It just didn't add up. Nuka and I looked around frantically, screaming out Unaaq's name at the top of our lungs. I kept expecting to see him come walking out of the fog. I didn't want to believe that our wise old guide was lost out there in the storm, lost without any sled dogs to bring him to safety.

We went back to Wyatt, carried him to the igloo, and wrapped him up in blankets to thaw him out. He's still out cold, but his pulse seems stronger and he's breathing well.

Nuka is worried sick about Unaaq and just went back outside to clear his head and tend to the dogs. As soon as Wyatt wakes up, we'll get the story. Hopefully, he has news of Unaaq's whereabouts.

GANNON

When Wyatt finally came to, the first thing he saw was me and Nuka standing over him. After what he'd been through he must have thought he was dreaming or something because his eyes opened real wide and started bouncing around in his head like he was trying to figure out where he was. Before he could even get a word out of his mouth, tears began streaming down his cheeks.

"You're safe, Wyatt," I said. "You made it."

I don't think Wyatt could believe it. I'm still having a hard time believing it myself.

Nuka and I made him some hot tea and gave him a biscuit, but his lips are so cracked and bloodied he cringed in pain at the first sip and didn't want any more. When he finally had the strength to speak, he told us the tragic story of Unaaq and their desperate struggle against the storm.

Honestly, I don't even know what to say. It's so hard to accept that Unaaq is actually gone. I mean, it just doesn't seem possible. Seriously, this whole thing is like another crazy nightmare that I need to wake up from. When we got the news, Nuka tried his best to be strong, but could only keep his sadness in check for so long. Soon, he started to cry. We all cried.

In all of our travels, I've had the opportunity to speak with elders from lots of different cultures, and even though their customs and rituals can be very different, most believe that there is some kind of heaven awaiting us after this life. It's impossible to say what's true and what's myth, really. I guess we won't know for certain until it's our turn to make that journey, but all these discussions have given me some ideas on the subject. The way I'd sum up my own belief is that when a person leaves this world, well, a part of them remains with us. I mean, they're alive in our memories and all, for sure, but I think it's more than that. It may sound crazy, but sometimes I can feel the presence of others, people who are no longer here. I think it's their spirits or whatever. And if that's true, or even partially true, Unaaq is definitely with us. He's with us and can feel all the love and appreciation we have for him. For real, I can easily imagine him standing before me with that big smile of his. There is definitely some comfort in that.

"My uncle was a great man," Nuka said, wiping his eyes. "I learned much from him over the years. It is very sad to lose him. However, this is our way of life. Unaaq explained it to me himself. He left his body on the ice. He would have wanted it no other way. A new journey has begun for him, but his wisdom and kindness will not be forgotten." Nuka looked to the sky. "Thank you for all you taught me, Uncle. I will miss you."

Finally, we were able to get a radio call through to Siorapaluk and learned that it should be clearing some over the next day, so we're planning to move out as soon as we're able.

It would be better if Wyatt could rest awhile longer and build up his strength before heading back into the cold, but we don't have that kind of time. His hands and feet are swollen like balloons. He has blisters all over his face and he's still in and out of consciousness. He needs medical attention as soon as possible, and we're down to the last of our food. Any more time out here and some of the Inughuit will succumb to starvation, so there's really no choice.

The dogs are all up and moving around and it seems they'll have enough strength to pull the sleds. The fact that Unaaq figured out what was ailing the dogs and came up with a remedy to heal them is just incredible. Truly, Unaaq is a lifesaver.

GANNON

Wyatt is wrapped like a cocoon on the front of Nuka's sled with his hands and feet double wrapped to keep them from getting any worse. We're moving west and the storm is blasting us full on from the side as it moves south, but overall we're running good and fast across hard ice where the wind has blown off much of the snow.

Way up here this time of year the sun doesn't really set, just dips real low on the horizon and then comes back up. The constant light makes it possible to continue sledding as long as we have the strength. We covered a lot of distance today. Sixty miles, I'm guessing. Maybe even 70. Who knows? Not really keeping track, just doing all we can to keep the dogs moving. We're hungry, running on adrenaline, and a little shaky, but determined to get to Siorapaluk.

GANNON
POSSIBLY OUR LAST STOP

The worst of the storm has moved to the south of us and there is no more weather approaching from the north that we can see. The sun, like a ripe orange, sits low on the horizon. Above us is this amazing purple-blue sky and much further out over the ocean are all these wispy stripes of red and pink. A sunset in the middle of the night!

"I believe Unaaq has made a nice painting in the sky for us," Nuka said.

"He sure has," I said.

"These colors are a sign that we are safe. Maybe it was Unaaq who cleared the way for us."

"I guarantee it was. Thank you, Unaaq."

We can't be far now and to be honest I didn't want to stop, but truth is I don't think I could have gone another mile without falling face down in the snow. Wyatt is only conscious for short bits of time. He's eaten very little, and doesn't say much when he's awake. He's just too weak.

Unaaq, my good friend, please see us through to the finish!

GANNON
THE FINAL PUSH TO SIORAPALUK

Coming around a mountainous point, we spotted a channel of water off in the distance. We hugged the shoreline where the ice was thicker, and as we ran I noticed some movement way out on the open water. At first I thought it might have been a family of walruses, but when I took out the binoculars for a closer look I was surprised to see one of the most unique creatures on the planet—the narwhal!

There must have been, I don't know, fifteen, maybe even twenty of them. All swimming together with their unicorn horns sticking up out of the water like a bed of needles. It was so awesome to get a glimpse of these rare and bizarre creatures, and under different circumstances we would have gone to the edge of the ice to get a closer look, but we didn't even break stride. At this point in our journey, we weren't stopping for anything.

Narwhals surfacing for air

Maybe an hour or so later the triangular roofs of Siorapaluk came into view. At the sight, everyone started to shout
and holler with pure joy! The thought that we were coming
to the end of this long and difficult journey was an incredible
relief and all at once I experienced an overwhelming release
of emotion. All the stuff I'd kept buried inside, I guess—the
fear and sadness, the exhaustion and excruciating pain, all
mixed with the sudden and immeasurable relief of knowing
that I was going to survive—it all just poured out of me. My
eyes filled with tears and I sobbed uncontrollably.

Village in the high Arctic

As the dogs pulled us to the edge of town, we were greeted by just about every person in Siorapaluk. Men, women, and children streamed out of houses and onto the snowy street, all with smiling faces and watery eyes, shaking hands and hugging one another. A chorus of sighs and laughter filled the air. Everyone was simply overjoyed to see their loved ones safe and sound after they'd been stranded on the ice for so long.

We carried Wyatt and a few others who were very weak into the village where the town's only nurse is now tending to them. We all hugged Suunia, and she told us how sorry she was to hear of Unnaq.

"He was a brave and wise man and will be sorely missed," she said. "Unfortunately, when you travel on the ice, there is always a chance you might not make it home. This is something every Greenlander understands. Given the severity of this storm, we must count ourselves lucky that more of you did not meet the same fate."

Suunia said this was the worst spring storm they've seen in over 50 years!

She's right. It's a total miracle any of us made it back.

WYATT

APRIL 23, 12:22 PM
SIORAPALUK, 77° 47' N 70° 38' W
12° FAHRENHEIT, -11° CELSIUS
SUNNY SKIES

Resting in a warm bed. Thankful to be alive and grateful for our friend Unaaq. The remedy he made saved the lives of 14 people who had been stranded for weeks. Rightfully so, Unaaq is a hero here in Siorapaluk. In his memory, they erected a cairn, which is a high pillar of round rocks stacked atop one another. Personally, I don't know that I'll ever get over what happened to us on the ice. I don't see how I could. It will be with me forever.

As for my condition, the top half of my little toe was black and swollen to twice its normal size. Nothing could be done to save it, so the nurse did what needed to be done. I'll be walking with a slight limp until it heals completely, and

I'm sure Gannon will come up with all kinds of nicknames for me now that I'm missing part of a toe. Considering what I endured, I am very fortunate I did not lose more.

Everyone else has been hydrated and fed and seems to be doing well. Gannon, Nuka, and I will stay in Siorapaluk for another day or two so that the nurse can monitor my recovery. Aside from the toe, she wants to keep an eye on several frostbitten spots on my left hand, foot, and face. Some have turned the slightest shade of gray, but I should recover. Once I am cleared by the nurse, we will be flown to Ilulissat to meet our parents, and Nuka will rejoin his family. All my parents know is that Gannon and I arrived safely in Siorapaluk. The rest we will tell them in person.

GANNON

I'll be totally honest, I was feeling pretty sick to my stomach at the thought of flying back to Illulissat and seeing my parents and all of Unaaq's relatives. I mean, what was I supposed to say to Unaaq's friends and family? How was I going to console them? I'd never been through this kind of thing. My stomach was turning over in flips the entire flight.

But, Nuka told us that Greenlanders know as well as anyone the dangers of an Arctic expedition. Like Suunia said, they understand that every time someone goes out on the ice they may not come back. That's life in the far North. Still, nothing could have prepared me for how calmly Unaaq's family and friends handled everything. Their serenity, it kind of blew me away. Over the course of this journey, the people of Greenland have given me a new appreciation of the things that are really and truly important in life—love and compassion, family and friendship. Bottom line, if you've got that, you've got everything.

This whole thing was a huge shock to my mom and dad. I mean, they were pretty much speechless after they picked us up and learned of everything that happened. And when my mom came across the letter Wyatt had written to us from his snow cave and read it aloud, there wasn't a dry eye in the room. We might have sat around all sad and red-eyed the rest of the day if Nuka's parents hadn't come to the hotel and insisted we all join them at their family's store for a "Greenlandic celebration."

A gathering had been planned to honor Unaaq's life, and I have to say that once it was underway, everyone was in such good spirits it was almost impossible to stay sad. Nuka's father, Makaali, who is Unaaq's younger brother, Erneq, and several of Unaaq's friends were telling all these great stories and singing and dancing and laughing and carrying on.

"We all grieve our loss and will miss Unaaq terribly," Makaali said to all those in attendance, "but today we must overcome our sadness. For today we celebrate my brother's wonderful and adventurous life. He is a hero who saved many people. Honor him with warm memories of his smiling face, his laugh, his compassion. I assure you, that is his wish."

After Makaali spoke, Wyatt and I approached him.

"We're so sorry for your loss," I said.

"I was stranded on the ice," Wyatt said. "Lost in the blizzard. Unaaq, he came back for me. He saved my life. I'll never . . ."

Wyatt got choked up and couldn't say anymore.

"It's okay, son," Makaali said, placing a hand on Wyatt's shoulder.

"When we were riding out the storm Unaaq told us a joke," I said, hoping to lighten the mood. "He said you found it on the internet. The one about the three Eskimos debating whose igloo was the coldest."

"Yes," Makaali said, bursting into a hearty laugh. "I remember the joke."

Wyatt even chuckled.

"He had us all rolling in the snow with laughter," I said.

"That's just like Unaaq," Makaali said. "Even when the situation was desperate, he knew how to lift people's spirits. Come now, let's celebrate this beautiful day in memory of my brother."

Afternoon sun shining in the bay

As Makaali requested, we rejoined the celebration, mingling among Unaaq's friends and family. I have to say, the setting for this celebration couldn't have been anymore spectacular, with all the jagged, sky-scraper sized icebergs adrift in the bay, the perfect blue sky overhead, the ice crystals shimmering like diamonds in the snow. Nuka's mom, Kunik, prepared reindeer meat over a steaming grill, and next to her was a long table piled high with treys of fish and potatoes and vegetables and deserts. The food looked so good it actually brought my appetite back.

Parked just outside the store was a traditional wooden sled just like the one we used on our journey. Friends and family were painting it all these bright colors and passing around a black marker so that everyone could write a message to Unaaq. Nuka told me the sled would remain outside the family store forever, a memorial to a brave and loving man. I sat alone in the snow for a while and thought about what to write. I didn't want to put down anything too heavy or sad or whatever, so I ended up writing this:

```
Unaaq,

See you on the flip side, buddy!

-Gannon
```

Cheesy, I know, but I bet it made Unaaq smile.

We're back at the hotel now, and I'm settled into my bed and warm and comfortable and to be honest, I'm feeling pretty decent considering all we've been through. I know this might sound "way out there" or whatever, but I could totally sense Unaaq's presence today. No joke, I really could. In some mystic way I know he's still with us, guiding our path just as he did on the ice.

WYATT

Ariel view, Southern Greenland

I am sure at some point in the near future I will be asked to explain the reason two young brothers with no Arctic experience would risk their lives to explore what many consider a barren wasteland of snow, ice, and rock. I am sure I will be asked to discuss the expedition's end, both tragic and heroic, where a life was lost and many others were saved. In time, I will be prepared to talk about these things. For now, all explanation related to these matters will be left to the writings within my journal.

As for what's next, we cannot say. I should mention, however, that my brother and I do intend to continue this business of travel and exploration. It is part of who we are, our true passion, and I honestly don't know what we would do with ourselves otherwise.

Once you have looked death squarely in the eyes and accepted that your time is up, life is changed. At this moment, flying high along the southeast coast of Greenland where rivers of ice snake their way into the Labrador Sea, I can tell that something within me is different. There is a strangeness to this day. It's as if my awareness has been heightened by a magnitude of one thousand. There is a new beauty to things big and small—to my parents and brother seated nearby, to the breathtaking view out the window, to the simple comfort I feel in this seat, to this Dash-7 airplane, which moves us so steadily through the air—life is magnificent and I am appreciating every bit of it.

Regarding our companions on this journey, I do have one thing left to write. I will never forget our great friend, Nuka, or his uncle, the heroic Arctic explorer, Unaaq. For saving my life I will remain in debt to him until the day I am called upon to begin my own journey in the afterlife. On that day, I hope that Unaaq is there to greet me. I hope that he is there so we can talk of this adventure. Most of all, I hope that he is there so I can thank him.

GANNON & WYATT's

The Alaskan Arctic

North Pole

Greenland

Denali

Baffin Island

Kodiak Island

Great Bear Rainforest

Cliffs of Moher, Ireland

Yellowstone Park

Niagara Falls

Stonehenge

Moab   Badlands

Paris, France

Grand Canyon

New Orleans

Barcelona, Spain

Everglades

Casablanca, Morocco

Tropic of Cancer

Bermuda Triangle

Big Island, Hawaii

The Caribbean

Galapagos Islands

The Amazon River

Machu Picchu, Peru

Tropic of Capricorn

Patagonia

TRAVEL MAP

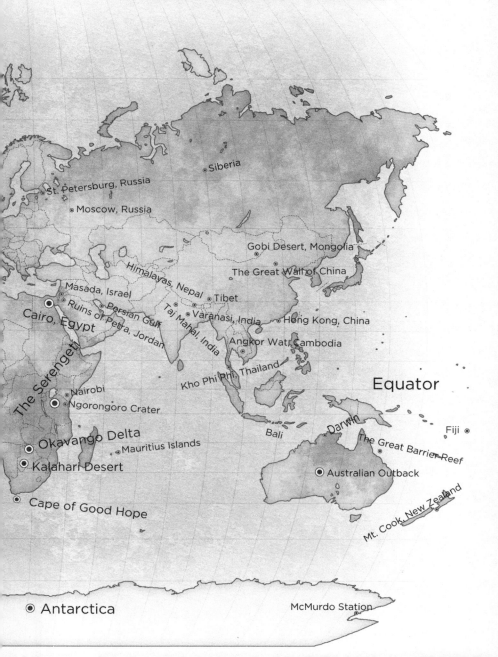

Siberia

St. Petersburg, Russia

Moscow, Russia

Gobi Desert, Mongolia

The Great Wall of China

Himalayas, Nepal

Masada, Israel

Tibet

Ruins of Petra, Jordan

Persian Gulf

Taj Mahal, India

Varanasi, India

Hong Kong, China

Cairo, Egypt

Angkor Wat, Cambodia

Kho Phi Phi, Thailand

The Serengeti

Equator

Nairobi

Ngorongoro Crater

Bali

Darwin

Fiji

Okavango Delta

Mauritius Islands

The Great Barrier Reef

Kalahari Desert

Australian Outback

Cape of Good Hope

Mt. Cook, New Zealand

Antarctica

McMurdo Station

AUTHORS' NOTE

There are places on earth so extraordinarily beautiful the mere act of being there gives rise to a spiritual awakening in the traveler. It is these places that inspire in us a lifelong desire to travel the globe, always searching for the next location that will leave us astonished by its splendor. Greenland is one such place.

Inevitably, such a profound travel experience sends you away with a deep affection for the place, its natural environment and the people who live there. The concerns of the people become that of the traveler. This happened to us in Greenland, where two issues were continually brought up in conversation: the preservation of Greenlandic culture and climate change.

Many Greenlanders we spoke with felt their way of life was misunderstood. Their culture, they said, was often dismissed as primitive and in need of modernization. Indeed, outside influence is already reshaping the country. After visiting the Greenland National Museum in Nuuk one rainy July afternoon, we walked back to our hotel in the center of town. Along the way, we passed high-rise office buildings, newly constructed condominiums, banks, an electronics store, and a clothing retailer carrying a variety of international brands. All were clear examples of how life in Greenland is already changing.

Of course, not all of these things are bad. Many Greenlanders actually appreciate some of the changes. As anthropologist Hugh Brody put it, the issue isn't traditional versus a modern way of life, but whether or not indigenous people are free to choose how they go about their lives.

As for climate change, Greenlanders do not need a scientific report to tell them what's happening. They are witnessing the impact of climate change with their own eyes. Temperatures in the Arctic are warming faster than anywhere else on earth. Waterways that used to freeze solid in the winter, no longer do. Storms are more severe, the ice sheet is melting, and sea levels are rising. Nature is in flux, disrupting the indigenous peoples' ability to hunt and fish and provide for their families.

Given this truth, it may be the indigenous people of the Arctic who sound the loudest alarm in the years to come, motivating the rest of the world to take the decisive action necessary to ensure the long-term health of our planet. In the *Travels with Gannon & Wyatt* books, we encourage young people to learn from the world's indigenous cultures. Their teachings might just provide the inspiration we need to reevaluate our own relationship with nature—this being the critical first step if we hope to make good on our responsibility to leave behind a cleaner, safer world for our children.

Gannon and Wyatt in Greenland

MEET THE "REAL-LIFE" GANNON AND WYATT

Have you ever imagined traveling the world over? Fifteen-year-old twin brothers Gannon and Wyatt have done just that. With a flight attendant for a mom and an international businessman for a dad, the spirit of adventure has been nurtured in them since they were very young. When they got older, the globetrotting brothers had an idea—why not share all of the amazing things they've learned during their travels with other kids? The result is the book series, Travels with Gannon & Wyatt, a video web series, blog, photographs from all over the world, and much more. Furthering their mission, the brothers also cofounded the Youth Exploration Society (Y.E.S.), an organization of young people who are passionate about making the world a better place. Each Travels with Gannon & Wyatt book is loosely based on real-life travels. Gannon and Wyatt have actually been to Greenland and run dog sleds on the ice sheet. They have kissed the Blarney Stone in Ireland, investigated Mayan temples in Mexico, and explored the active volcanoes of Hawaii. During these "research missions," the authors, along with Gannon and Wyatt, often sit around the campfire collaborating on an adventure tale that sets two young explorers on a quest for the kind of knowledge you can't get from a textbook. We hope you enjoy the novels that were inspired by these fireside chats. As Gannon and Wyatt like to say, "The world is our classroom, and we're bringing you along."

HAPPY TRAVELS!

Want to become a member of the
Youth Exploration Society
just like Gannon and Wyatt?

Check out our website. That's where you'll learn how to become a member of the Youth Exploration Society, an organization of young people, like yourself, who love to travel and are interested in world geography, cultures, and wildlife.

The website also includes:

Cool facts about every country on earth, a gallery of the world's flags, a world map where you can learn about different cultures and wildlife, spectacular photos from all corners of the globe, and information about Y.E.S. programs.

BE SURE TO CHECK IT OUT!
WWW.YOUTHEXPLORATIONSOCIETY.ORG

ACKNOWLEDGMENTS

We would like to pay tribute to the spirits of the grandparents that have gone before us; William Altor Gause, Sr., William Altor Gause, Jr., Mattie Alma Dean-Brock, Thomas Wyatt Davis, Thomas Franklin Davis, Alice Naomi Nesmith-Davis, Lebel Michael Wheeler, Mary Luella Fitzpatrick, Thomas Morgan Wheeler, Cecil Howard Fitzgibbon, Bertha Ellen Allinghom, Nancy Ann Fitzgibbon-Wheeler, Mary Louise Kippenberger, Clair Phillip Kippenberger, Opal Marie Paradise, John Nicholas Paradise, John Alexander Beckham, Joanna Ernestine Hock, Herbert Melville Hemstreet, and Jack Eugene Kippenberger.

As the Inuit proverb says, "Glorious it is when wandering time is come."

ABOUT THE AUTHORS

PATTI WHEELER, producer of the web series Travels with Gannon & Wyatt: Off the Beaten Path, began traveling at a young age and has nurtured the spirit of adventure in her family ever since. For years it has been her goal to create children's books that instill the spirit of adventure in young people. The Youth Exploration Society and Travels with Gannon & Wyatt are the realization of her dream.

KEITH HEMSTREET is a writer, producer, and cofounder of the Youth Exploration Society. He attended Florida State University and completed his graduate studies at Appalachian State University. He lives in Aspen, Colorado, with his wife and three daughters.

Make sure to check out the first three books in our award-winning series:

Botswana

Great Bear Rainforest

Egypt

Look for upcoming books and video from these and other exciting locations:

Ireland

Hawaii

Mexico

Australia

Iceland

The American West

Don't forget to check out our website:

WWW.GANNONANDWYATT.COM

There you'll find complete episodes of our award-winning web series shot on location with Gannon & Wyatt.

You'll also find a gallery with spectacular photographs from Greenland, Iceland, Egypt, the Great Bear Rainforest, and Botswana.

And wait, one more thing...

Check us out on Twitter, Pinterest, and make sure to "like" us on Facebook! With your parents permission, of course.

If you enjoyed Gannon and Wyatt's adventure in
Egypt, make sure to read the book that started it all . . .

TRAVELS WITH **GANNON & WYATT**

BOTSWANA

National Outdoor Book Award Winner
Nautilus Award Silver Medal Winner
Winner of Five Purple Dragonfly Book Awards
Moonbeam Children's Book Award Silver Medalist
Colorado Book Award Finalist

"Botswana has rarely had a portrayal that so accurately captures the physical
and emotional spirit of Africa . . . This is a brilliant first of what I hope will be
many books in a travel-novel series."
—*Sacramento Book Review*

Discover more adventures in . . .

TRAVELS WITH **GANNON & WYATT**

GREAT BEAR
RAINFOREST

"A groundbreaking series of adventurous stories like nothing else in children's
literature. Kids of all ages and from all backgrounds love these stories because
they are packed with action, humor, mystery, and fun adventures."
—Mark Zeiler, middle school language arts teacher, Orlando, Florida

MY JOURNAL NOTES

_____

_____

_____

_____

_____

_____

_____

_____

_____

_____

_____

_____

_____

_____

Station Nord

GREENLAND SEA

SIORAPALUK

BAFFIN BAY

UPERNAVIK

GREENLAND

ICE.

RE

ILULISSAT

IN ISLAND

DAVIS STRAIT

NUUK

LABRADOR SEA

ALASKA

ARCTIC OCEAN

ARCTIC CIRCLE

HUDSON BAY

CANAD